THE CHRISTMAS GIFT

A MAIL ORDER BRIDE LOVE STORY

OLIVIA POE

Cover Design by Covers and Cupcakes LLC

https://coversandcupcakes.com/

ABOUT THIS BOOK ...

THE CHRISTMAS GIFT

When her cruel uncle forces Grace into marriage with a Kansas farmer, she believes no man would want her unless he was paid to take her.

After her father's death, Grace Royce loses everything—her inheritance, her mother's precious jewelry, and her freedom.

Shipped west as a mail-order bride, she's convinced her new husband Daniel Carrington only married her for the dowry her uncle provided.

But Daniel never received any payment. He chose Grace, believing she wanted a fresh start. Now he's baffled by his beautiful wife who burns breakfast, faces down snakes with courage, yet acts like she's walking on eggshells around him.

As Grace learns farm life through hilarious disasters and growing confidence, she begins to trust Daniel's genuine kindness.

But when town gossips spread vicious rumors and the truth about her uncle's lies threatens everything, will their fragile love survive?

A heartwarming Christmas story of scattered pearls

made whole, second chances, and the healing power of true love.

Perfect for fans of mail-order bride romances, Christmas love stories, and characters who overcome trauma to find their happily ever after.

CHAPTER 1

BOSTON JULY 1885

The shadows hovered dark and low, forcing Grace to pause and allow her eyes to adjust to the gloom before she stepped into the study.

For two weeks, at the command of her uncle, the south-facing wall of windows had remained cloaked in heavy brocade curtains. Not a single ray of sunlight could penetrate the room.

The curtains were never closed when her father was alive, and the room was always full of sunshine. Grace's breath caught in her throat, and she was again reminded of how quickly things had changed with her father's death.

Blinking rapidly, forcing her eyes to adapt to the twilight of the room, Grace moved closer to her father's desk. Disheveled papers covered the top and hung out of the open drawers, stained accounting ledgers and open envelopes littered the floor.

"Such chaos! Father will have a fit!"

Grace knelt, gathering a packet of letters into her apron while reaching for an open accounting ledger face down on the patterned wool rug.

Her uncle's sharp, barked retort caused her to snatch her

hand back and unconsciously hide it under the clutch of correspondence in her lap.

"On your feet this minute, young lady! What this desk contains doesn't concern you! Considering your father has been buried for a fortnight, he has no say in the matter, and neither do you!"

Uncle spun on his heel, violently stabbing the floor near Grace with the silver metal tip of his walking cane. Venom radiated from the man in waves.

The man looming over her bore little resemblance to the good-natured uncle she remembered from childhood. Years of bitterness had carved deep lines around his mouth and between his heavy brows, giving his face an endless scowl.

He was a tall man, but thickened with age and privilege. He couldn't move without straining the buttons of his expensive waistcoat.

His gray hair, slicked back from a high forehead, gleamed in the dim light. Once fashionable, his thick mutton chop whiskers were now merely old and tired. His jowls quivered when he spoke.

The walking stick he wielded like a weapon was polished mahogany, topped with that silver handle. Given the quickness with which he moved, the cane was clearly more of an ornament than a necessity.

His eyes, small and dark beneath those bushy brows, held none of the warmth her father's eyes had possessed. The two men might have been brothers, but there the resemblance ended. Uncle's eyes glittered with a calculating coldness that made Grace's skin crawl.

Anguish gripped Grace and stole her voice. She kept her gaze on the floor as she rose to her feet, fiercely squinting to stop the scalding tears from spilling over.

She would not allow this man to upset her. This man was

her uncle, brother to her father, but she hadn't seen him in years, not until he rode into town two days before the funeral and took over her home.

From the looks of things, Uncle had ransacked her father's desk and files. Grace gave silent thanks she had had the foresight, days ago, to remove and hide the cash she knew her father kept for house expenses.

Her eyes slid sideways to an ornate Majolica urn displayed on the fireplace mantel. Its lid was missing, and it was clear someone had moved the vase from its original placement.

Grace bit the inside of her lip to keep from smiling. Father always hid money in the colorful jug, and Grace had removed the stashed coins and bills the same night she took the household money from the desk cash box.

Stepping closer to the desk, Grace carefully placed the bound packet of letters on one corner. A wave of icy fear swept through her, followed by a surge of fiery anger at what she saw. Gripping the edge of the desk for support, she willed herself to stay in control.

Automatically, her fingertips sought the pearl necklace she was wearing, grateful she had taken the time to put it on that morning. Knowing the necklace was around her neck calmed her somewhat, but not for long.

Alternate waves of anger and fear consumed Grace the more she stared at the top of the desk.

"What is my jewelry box doing here? Where is my mother's jewelry?" Grace fought to keep her voice calm as apprehension washed over her.

Someone had clearly forced the top of the box open. One hinge was broken, and the entire lid was askew.

Grasping the silver latch, she carefully pulled out the bottom drawer of the carved rosewood box.

Bare dark blue velvet winked back at her. Empty. Where

were her mother's watch and wedding ring? The remaining drawer was also empty.

Bile rose in Grace's throat, and she choked. A strangled whisper broke free. "Where is my jewelry?"

The look her uncle turned on her was pure animosity. Her next words died in her throat.

"There are bills to pay and accounts to settle. Your father suffered serious losses in the last few years in his investments, and I need money to settle accounts. I've taken an inventory of the house contents, and I must sell everything."

Grace's blood ran cold at the words coming from her uncle. Grace could see the man's lips moving, but the words he spoke were hard to hear, as if he were far away.

"Your jewelry was a nice find, and worth more than I thought." The man was almost cackling with glee.

Grace thought she was going to faint. The room was spinning around like a top, and her vision became blacker and blacker.

She hadn't heard right. Did her uncle say he had sold her jewelry? Her mother's precious necklaces and jewels, gifts from her husband and her parents? Jewelry she'd collected during her entire life, and left to Grace, her only daughter and child, upon her death. All of those mementos and reminders of her mother were gone?

Uncle's mouth was open and his lips were moving, spittle mixed with the prattle about bills, and debts, and obligations her father had run up that must be paid off.

The words washed over Grace like a roaring river.

Grace was in denial and didn't hear.

This magnificent house, the only home she'd ever known, full of valuable furnishings and rugs, was not enough to pay the creditors?

What in the world had her father done to amass such debt?

Grace had seen no hint of indebtedness in the household ledgers her father taught her to keep. Her father mentioned no problems with money while he was alive.

The two of them sat down together weekly with the household bookkeeping, her father verifying the entries and balancing of numbers Grace had entered.

Grace also worked on a few of his business ledgers, and never, in the many years she had been responsible for this work, had she ever seen anything in arrears.

"I don't believe you. I want to see the ledgers and a list of the names and balances owed to these people."

The words fell from her lips as her head lifted and her chin jutted out in defiance. Her thoughts whirling, Grace didn't realize she had spoken until her uncle lifted his cane and brought it down across the desktop, far too close to her fingers.

Her hand felt the wave of air from the crash of the cane, and a quick thrust of the walking stick sent the rosewood box crashing to the floor.

"It's none of your business, girl! It is my job to close the estate of my brother, and as a stupid girl, it is your place to step back and let a man do the job no woman is suited for!"

Grace stared at her uncle, feeling as if she were sinking and his forceful words were the ripples in the water closing over her head.

Uncle's eyes narrowed as they fixed on Grace's throat. "That necklace," he said, his voice dropping to a menacing whisper. "Take it off. Now."

Grace's hand flew instinctively to her mother's pearls, her fingers wrapping protectively around the smooth, warm stones. "No." The word came out stronger than she felt. "This was my mother's. You have no right—"

"I have every right!" Uncle's cane crashed against the desktop again. "Everything in this house belongs to the estate, and I am the executor. That includes whatever jewelry you're wearing."

"These pearls were a gift from my father to my mother on their wedding day. She put them around my neck herself before she..." Grace's voice broke, but she lifted her chin in defiance. "They're mine by right. You cannot have them."

Uncle's face twisted with rage. "You foolish girl! Do you think your sentimental attachments matter when there are debts to be paid? That necklace will bring enough to cover the dowry I must pay to find you a husband willing to take on such a burden."

Grace's blood turned to ice. "Dowry? What dowry?"

"Did you think any man would want to marry you for yourself?" Uncle's laugh was cruel. "A penniless orphan with no skills and expensive tastes? I must pay a farmer in Kansas to take you off my hands. And your mother's precious pearls will provide that payment."

"I won't give them to you." Grace backed toward the door, her hand still clutching the necklace. "Find another way to pay your debts."

Uncle moved with surprising speed for a man with a walking stick. He lunged forward, his gnarled hand grasping for the pearls around Grace's neck. "You will give them to me, or I will take them!"

Grace twisted away, but Uncle's fingers caught the strand. The delicate silk thread, worn from years of wear, snapped under the sudden tension. Pearls scattered across the floor like tears, bouncing and rolling into the shadows under furniture and into corners.

"No!" Grace fell to her knees, frantically trying to gather the scattered pearls, but Uncle's cane came down, blocking her reach.

"Look what your defiance has cost you," Uncle snarled,

kicking at the remaining visible pearls, sending them skittering further away. "Now you have nothing. Perhaps this will teach you the folly of opposing me."

Grace knelt on the floor, holding the broken clasp and a few pearls she had managed to save, tears streaming down her face as she watched her last connection to her mother disappear into the darkness of the room.

CHAPTER 2

That evening, after Uncle had retired to his rooms, Grace crept down the stairs in her bare feet. Her heart hammered against her ribs as she turned the study doorknob, praying it wouldn't creak.

The room was even darker now, lit only by pale moonlight filtering through gaps in the heavy curtains.

She had brought a small oil lamp and a cloth bag, determined to search every corner for the scattered pearls. Perhaps if she could find enough of them, she could have the necklace restrung. It wouldn't be the same—the silk cord her mother had worn was irreplaceable—but at least she would have something.

Grace set the lamp on the desk and dropped to her hands and knees, running her fingers along the baseboards and peering under the heavy furniture. The wool rug still bore the impression where she had knelt in fear, and her throat tightened at the memory.

"There," she whispered, spotting the soft gleam of a pearl wedged behind the leg of a wingback chair. The stone felt warm and smooth in her palm. Her heart lifted—if there was one, there might be more.

For nearly an hour, she searched. Under the desk, she found two more pearls. Behind the coal scuttle, another. One had rolled clear to the fireplace hearth. Each discovery felt like a small victory, a piece of her mother returned to her.

Grace had just spotted what looked like another pearl near the window when she heard footsteps in the hall. Panic seized her. She quickly extinguished the lamp and pressed herself against the wall behind the door, clutching the five pearls and broken clasp to her chest.

The footsteps passed by. Grace waited, counting her heartbeats, before lighting the lamp again. But as the flame flickered to life, her blood turned to ice.

The area where she had been searching—the entire space near the window where she had seen that last pearl—had been swept clean. Not just clean, but meticulously so. The dust patterns showed that someone had been here with a broom and dustpan.

Grace rushed to the other areas where she had not searched. The spaces under the furniture had been cleaned as well. Even the corner by the fireplace, where she was sure the pearls would roll to, now showed the telltale marks of careful sweeping.

"No, no, no..." she whispered, dropping to her knees again and running her hands frantically over the clean floor. But there was nothing. Someone had systematically collected and removed every remaining pearl.

Uncle had been here. He had picked up the pearls after she left, to ensure she could never recover the pieces of her mother's necklace.

Grace sank back on her heels, staring at the five small pearls in her palm—all that remained of her mother's wedding gift, the necklace that had been her most treasured possession. Five pearls and a broken clasp from a strand that had once held dozens.

She pressed the pearls against her heart, feeling their warmth, and made a silent promise to her mother. Somehow, somewhere, she would honor the love these pearls represented.

Uncle could steal her inheritance, force her into marriage, and sweep away the scattered remnants of her past, but he could not take her memories. He could not destroy what her mother had meant to her.

Grace carefully wrapped the five pearls and the broken clasp in her handkerchief, and tucked them deep into the pocket of her night robe.

Tomorrow she would sew them into the lining of her traveling dress, close to her heart, where Uncle could never find them.

As she crept back up the stairs, Grace felt something harden inside her heart. Uncle had taught her a valuable lesson tonight—there were people in this world who would take everything from you if you let them. She would let no one do that to her again.

THREE DAYS LATER, Grace sat stiffly in the same chair she had occupied during the pearl necklace confrontation. The study remained shrouded in darkness, the heavy curtains still blocking any hint of sunlight.

Uncle paced behind the massive desk, his walking stick banging sharply against the wooden floor.

"I have made the arrangements," Uncle announced without preamble. "You will leave on the morning train in three days' time. Your destination is Kansas."

Grace's hands remained folded in her lap, but her knuckles

were white. She had not spoken to her uncle since the incident with the pearls, and she would not give him the satisfaction of a response now.

"The man's name is Daniel Carrington. He owns a farm outside a town called Prescott." Uncle's voice carried a note of satisfaction. "He is in need of a wife, and I have assured him that you will serve his purposes."

Grace's jaw tightened, but she continued her silence.

Uncle stopped pacing and leaned against the desk, studying her with cold calculation. "He believes he is receiving a young woman eager for marriage and skilled in domestic duties. I saw no reason to correct his misconceptions."

This broke Grace's resolve. "You lied to him?"

"I presented you in the most favorable light possible," Uncle replied. "I am not concerned with what he discovers after the marriage is completed. At that point, I will have met my obligations, and he will be responsible for you."

"And what did you tell him about the dowry?" Grace's voice was tight with unshed tears.

Uncle's smile was predatory. "Ah yes, the dowry. I explained that your family's recent... financial difficulties... required a more modest arrangement. Mr. Carrington was understanding. For the sum of three hundred dollars, he agreed to take you as his bride."

Grace felt the blood drain from her face. "Three hundred dollars? You're paying him to marry me?"

"I am paying him to remove you from my care and provide you with a home and livelihood. It is more than you deserve, considering the burden you represent."

"But the jewelry you stole—my mother's jewelry—that was worth far more than three hundred dollars!"

Uncle's expression hardened. "I explained that jewelry was sold to settle your father's debts. The three hundred dollars comes from the sale of this house and its contents. Consider it your inheritance."

Grace suddenly stood, her chair scraping against the floor. "My inheritance? You've stolen everything that was rightfully mine, and now you're paying someone to take me away so you don't have to deal with me anymore!"

"Lower your voice," Uncle commanded, raising his cane in warning. "You will accept this arrangement with gratitude, or you will find yourself on the street with nothing. Mr. Carrington is a respectable man offering you a respectable home. Many women in your position would consider themselves fortunate."

"My position?" Grace's voice shook with rage and hurt. "The position you've put me in by stealing my inheritance and destroying my life?"

"The position your father put you in with his poor investments and reckless spending!" Uncle slammed his cane against the desk. "I am cleaning up his mess, and that includes finding a solution for his spoiled daughter."

Grace stared at him, seeing for the first time the depth of his hatred for her father, and for her. "You've hated us all along, haven't you? Father was successful, so Father had more money. You couldn't wait for Father to die so you could take everything he had and get rid of me."

Uncle's silence was answer enough.

"What if I refuse to go?" Grace asked.

"Then you will leave this house tomorrow with whatever you can carry, and you will make your own way in the world. No references, no money, no family connections to help you." Uncle's voice was flat and final. "The choice is yours—marriage to a farmer in Kansas, or destitution on the streets. Choose wisely."

Grace felt the walls of her world closing in around her. She thought of Chloe, the only person left who cared about her, and of the scattered pearls still hidden somewhere in this room—pearls she would never see again.

"When do I leave?"

"The train departs at eight o'clock Thursday morning. You will pack one trunk with your clothes and essential items. Nothing more. Mr. Carrington has been informed to expect you in Prescott on Saturday afternoon."

Numb, Grace nodded and moved toward the door.

"Grace." Uncle's voice stopped her at the threshold. She turned back to face him. "I suggest you learn quickly how to be a proper farm wife. Mr. Carrington paid good money for a helpmate, not a burden. Don't disappoint him the way your father disappointed everyone."

Grace left the room without another word, but Uncle's ultimate cruelty echoed in her mind as she climbed the stairs to her room.

In three days, she would board a train to marry a stranger who had paid for her. The knowledge burned in her chest like a brand, marking her as unwanted, worthless—bought and paid for like livestock at market.

CHAPTER 3

Fatigue weighed down her entire body like a bag of stones. The burden she was shouldering felt so heavy she stumbled when her toe caught a small ripple in the rug at the bottom of the staircase.

Lurching to one side, Grace grabbed the banister to keep from falling.

Staring at the contrast her white gloves made against the dark mahogany wood, Grace forced herself to focus.

Slowly breathing in and out, she willed her hammering heart to quiet in her chest and the rushing noise in her ears to subside.

Bit by bit, Grace cleared her head and straightened her spine. Standing tall, her slim fingers gripped the hem of her waistcoat and tugged nonexistent wrinkles from the cloth.

She was a Royce, and her upbringing did not allow weakness. Her father would be very disappointed in her if he could see her now.

Father... at the thought of her honorable father, dead now almost a month, her breath caught. Grace felt hot tears bubble up under the surface as she swallowed the lump in her throat.

Grace reminded herself she could do this, and she would do this. She would not bring shame to the Royce name.

She automatically turned toward the wall mirror to check her appearance. She did not see rosy cheeks reflected back at her. Instead, she saw the faded impression on the wall where an ornate mirror had hung for years.

Her gloved fingers floated through the air, reaching for the floral wallpaper while tracing the faded outline of the missing looking glass.

Snatching her hand back, Grace clenched the lapels of her cloak. The enormity of the situation she was facing suddenly hit her. Her knees threatened to buckle, and she sat down hard on the wooden steps.

Eyes flooded with tears, Grace brought the tips of her fingers to blot the corners of her eyes, only to see the small hole in the fingertip of the white glove.

She opened her mouth to call for Chloe but snapped it shut before making a sound. There was no Chloe to call anymore.

The golden-haired girl with her ever-escaping curls and rosy-cheeked prettiness had been dismissed along with the rest of the household staff when Uncle sold the house.

At seventeen, Chloe had been so much more than a housemaid: she'd been half lady's maid, half confidante, the sister Grace had never had.

For three years, Chloe had spent her mornings helping Grace dress and arrange her hair, her afternoons assisting with correspondence and mending, and her evenings sharing whispered conversations that blurred the lines between servant and friend.

Grace had never stood on ceremony, and Chloe's gentle nature, bright blue eyes sparkling with intelligence, and quick wit had made her irreplaceable.

Now she was gone, like everything else. The house stood empty and silent, and Grace was utterly alone.

Chloe was yet another reminder of so much that was wrong and why she was in the predicament she was in.

Grace Royce couldn't help it. Overwhelmed, she lowered her head and cried without making a sound.

PULLING a pocket watch from his vest, the old man turned to the office window, catching the watch face in a beam of sunlight and pretending to check the time. His fidgeting fingers ran up and down the edge of his lapel.

This young lady was a sharp one, just like her father. Best to humor her and do what he could to ease her mind and get her out of his office, lest she go elsewhere to make inquiries and start delving into issues better left alone. Issues that could spell trouble.

Pivoting around to face Grace, he pasted a smile on his face and waved his hand through the air.

"Your father was a reputable businessman, and very helpful to me and many others over the years."

With a grunt, the man pushed his girth into a wooden chair, his weight causing the chair to shudder and move back a few inches from the edge of a massive desk.

He reached out and picked up the slip of paper Grace had presented him with a few minutes earlier.

"Ah, yes, you are right, young lady. This chit notates a small amount due your father, when he was kind enough to advance money to me when I requested his assistance. Frankly, this amount is so small I deemed it inconsequential, and knew your father and I would settle up one evening over a smoke and perhaps a brandy."

The man continued to finger the slip of paper, pretending to be perplexed for the benefit of the young woman sitting across the desk from him.

"May I ask how you came to have this, and not your uncle? Your uncle settled your father's estate, did he not? Is your father's house not sold, his own credit obligations cleared by the monies your uncle received from property sales?"

Grace squirmed, uncomfortable under the hard gaze directed her way. She didn't expect this line of questioning, but she was a thinker, and fast on her feet.

"This was in one of the household ledgers, and I found it during the time Father's study was being cleaned out. I laid it aside, simply forgot about it during the confusion of the last many weeks. I found the note again a few days ago, and came to prevail upon your generosity and good name and collect what was due my father."

Grace spoke demurely, purposely lowering her eyes and pulling a hand-held fan from her purse. She had found the IOU in the Majolica vase, wrapped in crisp $20 and $50 bills her father had stowed there for emergencies.

Grace had a sudden thought: what if she had made a mistake coming here? What if the debenture had already been paid, and she was wrong in her attempt to collect? How did this man know what her uncle had sold and done to settle the estate? Did this man have contact with her uncle, and was this attempt to collect a debt going to backfire on her?

Slowly fanning her face to hold down the heat she felt rising up her neck, Grace lifted her gaze and smiled sweetly at the man across the desk.

"I know my father only did business with reputable businessmen, and I knew you would pay this note if I brought it to you. As I'm sure you've heard, I am leaving town soon, and any financial assistance you can give me in paying this debt to my father will assist me on my journey."

The man pushed the fingertips of both hands together and used his mammoth stomach as a resting place. The best thing to do would be to pay this woman and get her out of his office.

He knew well what the uncle was capable of, and what the uncle had done. He didn't need that rascal finding out about this debt and coming around for payment himself.

"There is a wedding in your near future, is there not?"

The man reached into a desk drawer and removed a small leather purse. He did not want to take a chance on writing a check and sending the young woman to the bank.

Looking up after she didn't answer his question, he was startled to see Grace's face void of color.

His hand hesitated before counting out five $50.00 bills. He counted the bills twice to himself, added one extra bill, and folded them in half. He pointed the bundle of money towards Grace.

Plucking the debt note from the desktop, he hurriedly wrote the date and "cash paid" across the top. Fanning the paper in the air for a moment to speed the drying of the ink, he then slipped the paper under his desk blotter.

Rising from his desk took the effort of a beefy hand on each chair arm and a push. "Let me see you out," he grunted.

Jumping to her feet, Grace tucked the cash into the inside pocket of her reticule. "Thank you very much, sir. I can see myself out. Good day."

The man moved to the window again, peering down at Grace as she crossed the street and hurried along the sidewalk, skirting the crowd milling between the vegetable stalls.

"James!" The man's call to his assistant was urgent. "James!"

Jotting instructions on a piece of paper, the man held up the note as James entered his personal office.

"James, I want you to visit the train depot and buy a ticket that includes a sleeping car. Deliver the ticket to this address. Did you see the young lady who just left my office?"

James snapped to attention, quickly skimming the note paper passed to his hands.

"Yes, sir, I noticed the young lady. She's quite a looker, sir."

The older man snarled, "Comments like that are unnecessary. Your job is to buy the ticket and deliver it to the young lady that just left my office. Make sure you put the ticket in her hands, and her hands only. Don't stay long; don't engage her in conversation. I do not need her back here asking questions. Deliver the ticket and then go. But keep your eyes open as to what you can see around that house."

Nodding his head to show he understood his employer's instructions, James scurried from the room.

CHAPTER 4

The two young women stood facing each other on the train platform, tears glistening on cheeks as they clung to one another.

The sudden, sharp wail of the train whistle piercing the air caused Grace to jump. To cover a sudden overwhelming feeling of dread, she giggled as she gave Chloe one last quick hug.

"Ah, the adventure that awaits! Chloe, I'll write to you, and you write to me, too! I'll tell you what the town is like. I really wish I could take you with me now. I really do."

Chloe's eyes were bright with unshed tears, her voice tight. "Grace, I will write, and I will miss you terribly. I know you will be all right."

Chloe pressed a small wicker basket into Grace's hands. "I've packed a few things for your trip. Mom insisted on making a few extras to send with you. It calms Mom's heart to know you'll have food to tide you over if you can't get to the dining car."

Grace hugged her former employee and close friend one more time, sad to know this part of her life was coming to an end. Grace turned and boarded the train. Another chapter was beginning.

~

THE CARRIAGE DOOR SLID OPEN, just far enough for a young woman to stick her head in. Grace turned from the window and was met with a wide grin.

"Good morning!"

Large emerald-green eyes beamed at Grace. The young woman radiated a cheerfulness that was infectious. Startled, Grace stared for a minute before she automatically smiled back.

Pushing the door open wider, the young woman pulled in a large suitcase from the train aisle and dropped to her knees, grunting as she wedged the bag under the bench seat. She quickly stowed two smaller satchels next to the case. She kept her purse glued to her side.

Plopping onto the seat across from Grace, she laughed out loud and stuck out her hand.

"I'm Cassie!"

Grace slowly raised her gloved hand and grasped Cassie's tanned, bare hand. "It's a pleasure to meet you, Cassie. I'm Grace."

With the lush countryside rushing past the windows as a backdrop, the two young women chatted and got to know one another.

Both girls were mail-order brides, traveling to meet a new husband and establish a new home. Cassie took for granted that Grace had picked her beau from a newspaper advertisement the same way she had, and out of embarrassment Grace didn't clarify her situation.

Grace was too ashamed to admit she had been forced from

her previous station in life and lost everything near and dear to her because of her father's debts.

As Cassie kept up a torrent of never-ending chitchat, Grace removed her gloves and tucked them into her purse. The food basket Chloe had given her sat next to her purse on the floor under the seat.

"Let's see what I have here," Grace straightened as she pulled the wicker basket onto her lap, smiling at Cassie but interrupting the girl's stream of chatter describing her courtship by postal letter.

Grace was determined to steer the conversation away from weddings and new husbands.

Carefully folding back the colorful scrap of fabric tucked around the hamper contents, Grace caught a whiff of cinnamon, cloves, and a hint of vanilla. A warm, spicy smell filled the sleeping car. The sudden rumble of her stomach warned Grace she had skipped eating breakfast.

"Oh, look!" Cassie jumped to her feet, peering over the basket handle. "Is that apple hand pie?" She couldn't contain her excitement as she reached for the food.

Suddenly remembering her manners, Cassie snatched her hand back as her face turned bright red. She sat back down, clasping her fingers together in her lap, hoping that Grace would share.

"I'm sure this is mincemeat pie, but there are two shiny red apples, sugar cookies, and, oh my! An orange and a banana!" Grace displayed the half-moon yellow fruit on her open palm.

Cassie's eyes grew round. "A banana? What does it taste like?"

"You've never eaten a banana?"

Cassie shook her head, her eyes wider yet.

With a flick of her wrist, Grace snapped open the end of the banana and cleanly pulled off sections of the peel. She broke the fruit in half and placed the pieces on a white linen napkin spread out on the bench seat. Next to each banana piece, Grace placed a mincemeat hand pie.

"Go ahead, taste the banana! I hope you like it!" Grace urged Cassie to help herself to the food.

Eyes shining, Cassie sank her teeth into the banana and swooned.

Cassie meticulously removed the last of the crumbs from the napkin before folding it and handing it to Grace. "Thank you, Grace. I was hungry, and the food was delicious. I was so worried about missing the train I didn't take the time to eat breakfast this morning."

Tucking the napkin back into the hamper, Grace studied the young face. She had a sudden feeling of kinship with Cassie.

It was clear they came from vastly different stations in life, but the two of them were not that much different, not at all.

ON THE SECOND evening of her journey, Grace ventured to the dining car. Her stomach had been growling for hours, and Chloe's gift basket was nearly empty.

The car swayed as the train rounded a curve, and Grace gripped the backs of seats to steady herself as she made her way down the narrow aisle.

The dining car was cozy, filled with the gentle sounds of cutlery and hushed chatter. Grace hesitated in the doorway, conscious of her simple traveling dress among the well-dressed passengers. A kind server approached her.

"Table for one, miss?"

Before Grace could answer, a cheerful voice called out, "Grace! Over here!"

Cassie sat at a small table near the window and waved

enthusiastically. Across from her sat a middle-aged woman with silver-streaked hair pulled back in a neat chignon. The woman's traveling dress was well-made but practical, and her eyes held a warmth that reminded Grace of her mother.

"Please join us," the woman smiled as Grace approached. "I'm Mrs. Eleanor Hartford. Cassie has been telling me about your journey."

Grace slid into the seat beside Cassie, grateful for the company. "It's a pleasure to meet you, Mrs. Hartford."

"Eleanor, please. We're all travelers here, thrown together by circumstance." Eleanor's grin was genuine. "Cassie tells me the two of you are heading to Kansas as mail-order brides. How exciting for you both!"

Grace felt heat rise in her cheeks. "Yes, ma'am."

Eleanor studied Grace's face with kind but perceptive eyes. "You don't sound as enthusiastic as most young women in your situation. Are you having second thoughts?"

"Oh, no!" Cassie interjected quickly. "Grace is just more reserved than I am. She's told me all about her intended, Daniel Carrington. He sounds like a wonderful man."

Grace forced a smile, hating the lie but unable to correct it. How could she explain she was being shipped off like unwanted cargo to a man who had been paid to take her?

"I'm escorting two other young ladies to Colorado," Eleanor said, gracefully changing the subject. "They're in their compartment, resting. This is my third such journey this year. It's become quite a calling for me, helping young women find new lives in the West."

"Do they..." Grace hesitated, then forced herself to continue. "Do they all work out? The marriages, I mean?"

Eleanor's expression grew thoughtful. "Most do, in time. The key is remembering that love isn't always immediate, child. Sometimes it grows slowly, like a garden carefully tended. The couples who succeed are those who approach marriage as partners, not adversaries."

Grace nodded, but Eleanor's words felt hollow. How could she be a partner to a man who had to be paid to marry her?

~

THE NEXT MORNING, Grace and Cassie made their way to the dining car for breakfast.

Near the windows, a young family was struggling with their meal. Two little boys, perhaps four and six years old, were bouncing in their seats while their harried mother tried to maintain order.

"Tommy, sit down," the woman's voice was weary. "And Peter, stop throwing your biscuit."

As if summoned by her words, a piece of biscuit came flying through the air, landing squarely in Grace's coffee cup. The splash sent drops of coffee across the sleeve of her white blouse.

"Peter Carrington!" the mother gasped, mortified. "I am so sorry, miss. Here, let me—"

Grace froze. "Carrington?" She repeated, her voice frail.

"Yes, we're the Carrington family from Kansas City, Missouri. Oh dear, your lovely blouse..." The woman frantically dabbed at Grace's sleeve with her napkin.

"Are you... do you know Daniel Carrington?" Grace's heart was pounding.

The woman paused in her cleaning efforts. "Why yes, he's my husband's cousin. How do you know Daniel?"

Grace felt the blood drain from her face. These were Daniel's family members. His cousins. She was looking at the children who would be her... her cousins once removed, she supposed.

"I... yes, I'm..." Grace couldn't seem to form the words.

Cassie leaned forward. "Grace is going to marry your cousin, Daniel Carrington! Isn't that wonderful?"

The woman's eyes widened, and her face lit up with delight. "You're Grace! Oh my goodness, Daniel's bride! He's told us much about you in his letters." She turned to call to her husband. "Robert Lee! Come meet Daniel's fiancée!"

A tall man with kind eyes approached their table. "Well, I'll be. You're the young lady who's captured our Daniel's heart." He extended his hand. "I'm Robert Carrington, and this is my wife, Diane. And these two rascals are Tommy and Peter."

Numb, Grace shook his hand, overwhelmed by the couple's warmth and excitement. They talked as if Daniel were eager for this marriage, as though he had chosen her rather than getting paid to marry her.

"Daniel is so looking forward to meeting you," Diane gushed. "He's been preparing the house, making sure everything is perfect. He even planted flower gardens around the porch because he hoped you'd like them."

Grace's throat tightened. "He... he planted flowers?"

"Oh yes! Roses and morning glories and sweet peas. He said, 'Any woman brave enough to travel west to marry me deserves to have something beautiful waiting for her'."

Robert chuckled. "My cousin has always been a romantic at heart, though he'd deny it if you asked him. He's been like a nervous schoolboy ever since he decided to find a wife."

"Decided?" Grace repeated. "He decided?"

"Well, yes," Diane said, looking puzzled by Grace's confusion. "After his neighbor's mail-order marriage worked out so well, Daniel decided he wanted to find a wife, too. He said he was tired of living alone on that big farm."

Grace felt as though the train car was spinning around her. Daniel had chosen to find a mail-order bride? He hadn't been approached by Uncle with an offer to take a penniless, unwanted niece off his hands?

"Are you feeling well, dear?" Diane asked with concern. "You look quite pale."

"I... excuse me," Grace managed, rising unsteadily from her seat. "I'm afraid I need some air."

She fled the dining car, leaving Cassie to make her apologies, and stumbled back to her compartment. Her mind was reeling with confusion. Her uncle had either lied to her about the arrangement, or Daniel's family didn't know the truth about the payment.

But if Daniel had truly chosen to find a wife, why would Uncle need to pay him anything?

CHAPTER 5

PRESCOTT, KANSAS

The train's whistle shrieked as it pulled into Prescott station on Saturday. Grace's stomach was tied in knots as she gathered her belongings. Cassie squeezed her hand encouragingly.

"You'll be fine," Cassie's voice was firm. "And just think—after today, you'll be Mrs. Daniel Carrington!"

Grace managed a weak smile as they made their way to the platform. The air was muggy and carried the scent of wood smoke and burning coal. Prescott was smaller than she had expected, but the station was bustling with activity.

"There!" Cassie pointed excitedly. "That tall man by the wagon—he keeps looking at the train. That must be your Daniel!"

Grace followed Cassie's gaze and felt her breath catch. Daniel Carrington was indeed tall, with broad shoulders that spoke of hard physical work.

His dark hair was neatly combed, and he wore Sunday church clothes and a nervous expression that made him look younger than she had expected. He held his hat in his hands, turning it anxiously as he scanned the disembarking passengers.

"He's quite handsome," Cassie nodded approvingly. "And look how nervous he is! He must be so excited to meet you."

Grace watched as Daniel's eyes passed over her without recognition, clearly looking for someone else entirely. Of course! He had no idea what she looked like, just as she had known nothing about him.

"Grace Royce?"

She turned to find the stationmaster approaching with a clipboard. "Yes?"

"Your husband-to-be asked me to watch for you. He's right over there." The man gestured toward Daniel, who had moved closer when he heard her name called.

Daniel approached slowly, his eyes taking in her appearance with obvious relief. Whatever he had been expecting, Grace apparently met his standards.

"Miss Royce?" His voice was deep and pleasant, with a slight nervousness that put Grace more at ease.

"Yes, Mr. Carrington? Daniel?"

He nodded and stepped closer, close enough that she could see his eyes were a warm brown. "I hope your journey wasn't too difficult. I know it's a long way from..." He paused, looking uncertain.

"Boston, Massachusetts." Grace supplied, realizing how little she knew about the man, and he her.

"Boston." he repeated. "Yes. Well, welcome to Kansas. To Prescott." He seemed to remember his manners and gestured toward her trunks. "Let me get your luggage loaded."

As Daniel and the porter loaded her trunks into his wagon, Grace said goodbye to Cassie, promising to stay in touch. Eleanor Hartford appeared at her elbow, giving her a motherly hug.

"Remember what I told you, dear," Eleanor was slow to let go. "Gardens take time to grow and need regular tending."

Then Grace found herself seated beside Daniel on the wagon bench, her hands folded tightly in her lap as they rolled out of the train station and on the road toward her new life.

As they approached the main street of Prescott, Daniel slowed the wagon and cleared his throat nervously. "Grace, I should explain about... about the arrangements for this evening."

Grace's stomach tightened. "Arrangements?"

"Well, the wedding." Daniel's ears turned red. "I've spoken with Reverend Shoemaker at the Methodist church. He's agreed to perform the ceremony this afternoon at four o'clock, if that's agreeable to you. I thought... well, it seemed proper to have everything official before..." He trailed off, clearly embarrassed.

"Of course," Grace said quickly, though her heart was racing. She had known this moment would come, but somehow the reality of it felt sudden and overwhelming. "That's very proper of you."

Daniel looked relieved. "Mrs. Clarkson — she's my neighbor — she's offered to help you prepare. There is a room above the general store where you can rest and... well, she thought you might want to change clothes or freshen up after your long journey."

"That's very kind of her." Grace was grateful for the thoughtfulness, even as her mind reeled with the swiftness of it all. In a few hours, she would be married to the man sitting beside her. Her arms and legs were leaden at the thought, and she was unable to move.

"The hotel has a dining room," Daniel continued, his nervousness evident in the way he gripped the reins. "I thought we could have dinner there after the ceremony. It's not fancy, but it's the nicest place in town. We will have a proper wedding dinner before we go to the farm."

Grace nodded, touched by his efforts to make the day special despite the unusual circumstances. "You've thought of everything."

~

BY THREE-THIRTY THAT AFTERNOON, Grace stood in a small room above the Prescott General Store, staring at her reflection in a cracked mirror.

Mrs. Clarkson, a plump woman with kind eyes and graying hair, bustled around her making final adjustments to Grace's dress.

"There now, dear," Mrs. Clarkson smoothed the skirt of Grace's best Sunday dress—a deep blue wool that brought out her eyes. "You look lovely. That blue is perfect on you."

Grace touched the simple cameo at her throat, one of the few pieces of jewelry Uncle hadn't found. Hidden beneath her corset, sewn carefully into the lining, were the five precious pearls and broken clasp—her mother's memory pressed close to her heart.

"Are you nervous, dear?" Mrs. Clarkson asked gently.

"Yes," Grace admitted. "I suppose all brides are nervous."

"Especially when they're marrying a man they've just met," Mrs. Clarkson's tone was understanding. "But Daniel's a good man, Grace. One of the finest in these parts. He'll treat you well."

Grace nodded, wishing she could explain that her nervousness came not from marrying a stranger, but from the crushing knowledge that he had been paid to take her. How did one begin a marriage knowing you were a purchased burden?

~

The little Methodist church was simple but clean, with polished wooden pews and clear glass windows that caught the rays of the late afternoon sun.

A few dozen townspeople had gathered; apparently, word of the mail-order bride's arrival had spread quickly through Prescott.

Grace walked down the short aisle on the arm of Mr. Clarkson, who had kindly offered to give her away.

Daniel waited at the front in a clean white shirt and dark suit, his hair freshly combed and his hands clasped nervously behind his back. When he saw her, his face lit up with what appeared to be genuine admiration.

Reverend Shoemaker, a thin man with gentle eyes, smiled warmly as Grace reached the front of the church.

"Dearly beloved," he began, "we are gathered here in the sight of God to join this man and this woman in holy matrimony."

The familiar words washed over Grace as she stood beside Daniel, acutely aware of his height and the clean scent of soap that clung to him. When it came time for the vows, Daniel's voice was steady and sure.

"I, Daniel, take thee, Grace, to be my wedded wife, to have and to hold from this day forward, for better, for worse, for richer, for poorer, in sickness and in health, to love and to cherish, till death us do part."

Grace's voice wavered slightly as she repeated the same words, meaning them despite her fears. Whatever the circumstances that brought them together, she would try to be a good wife to this man.

She was a Royce, and a Royce kept their word.

When Reverend Shoemaker pronounced them husband and

wife, Daniel turned to her with a shy smile. "May I?" he asked quietly.

Grace nodded, and Daniel leaned down to brush his lips gently against hers. It was brief and chaste, but Grace felt something flutter in her chest at the contact.

"Ladies and gentlemen," Reverend Shoemaker announced to the small gathering, "I present to you Mr. and Mrs. Daniel Carrington."

THE COZART HOTEL dining room was indeed the finest establishment in Prescott, with white tablecloths and real china plates. Daniel had reserved a small table by the window, and he pulled out Grace's chair with careful courtesy.

"Thank you." Grace was still adjusting to the reality that she was now Mrs. Daniel Carrington. Grace Carrington. The name felt strange on her tongue.

"I hope you like the food," Daniel said as they settled at their table. "Mrs. Romano is the head cook here, and she is known for her fried chicken and apple pie."

The meal was simple but well-prepared, though Grace found herself too nervous to eat much. Daniel seemed to understand, making easy conversation about the town and pointing out landmarks through the window.

"That's the old schoolhouse," he said, gesturing toward a small white building just past the Methodist church. "The teacher, Miss Crawford, boards with the Shoemakers. She's been asking for someone to help with the younger children, if you're interested in such things."

Grace looked up from her barely touched plate. "You think I might teach?"

"Well, your letters mentioned that you were well-educated.

I thought perhaps..." Daniel paused, studying her face. "Unless that doesn't appeal to you?"

"Oh no, it does." Grace was touched that he had thought about ways she might contribute to the community. "I would like that very much."

Daniel smiled, and Grace felt that flutter again. Perhaps this arrangement wouldn't be entirely without hope.

As the evening drew to a close, Daniel paid for their meal and offered Grace his arm. "It's a few miles buggy ride to the farm, but we'll get there before dark. It's time I took my wife home."

Grace placed her hand on his arm, feeling the solid strength beneath the fabric of his coat. For better or worse, she was now Mrs. Daniel Carrington.

Whatever came next, at least she had a roof over her head, and she was no longer alone.

CHAPTER 6

For the first few miles, they traveled in awkward silence. The countryside was beautiful—rolling hills covered in trees and fields of grain, split-rail fences, and large farms. Grace stole glances at Daniel's profile as he concentrated on driving.

Daniel cleared his throat. "I hope you'll like the house. I've tried to get it ready for you. Mrs. Clarkson, that helped you today, also helped me with the... the feminine touches."

"That was very thoughtful of her," Grace managed.

"I wasn't sure what you'd like." Daniel's words were coming faster now. He was clearly nervous. "Your letters didn't say much about your particular likes and dislikes."

Grace's heart sank. Uncle must have written letters pretending to be her. What lies had he told this man?

Grace felt herself getting smaller. "I hope I won't be too much of a disappointment," she mumbled.

Daniel pulled the wagon to a stop and turned to look at her fully.

"Disappointment? Miss Royce—Grace—I don't think you

understand. I'm the one who should be worried about disappointing you. You're a lady of refinement, and I'm just a farmer. I hope... I hope you won't regret coming here."

Grace stared at him in confusion. This was not the attitude of a man who had been paid to take an unwanted burden off someone's hands. This was the nervousness of a man who genuinely hoped to make a good impression.

"The letters you received," Grace chose her words carefully, "what did they tell you about me?"

Daniel's cheeks reddened. "Well, they mentioned you were well-educated and came from a good family. And that you were looking for a fresh start in the West after some family difficulties. I appreciated your honesty about that—we all have things in our past we'd rather leave behind."

Grace felt tears prick her eyes. Uncle's letters had painted her as someone seeking a new beginning, not as cargo to be disposed of. But if that was true, why had Uncle insisted Daniel was being paid to take her?

"I should warn you," Daniel continued, misinterpreting her tears, "I'm not much for fancy living. The house is comfortable, but it's not a mansion. And farm life is hard work. I hope that won't be too much of a change for you."

"No," Grace said softly, thinking of the scattered pearls and Uncle's cruelty. "I think I'm ready for hard work."

Daniel smiled broadly, taking her hand in his. Grace felt that flutter in her chest again.

"In that case," he said, "welcome home, Grace."

As they continued toward the farm, Grace felt a tiny spark of hope kindle in her heart. Perhaps her new life wouldn't be the punishment Uncle had made it seem. Perhaps despite everything she might find something good here after all.

~

Grace woke to the sound of roosters crowing and the distant lowing of cattle.

For a moment, she lay still in the unfamiliar bed, disoriented by the pale morning light filtering through windows she didn't recognize.

Then reality crashed over her—she was Mrs. Daniel Carrington now, in her new home in Prescott, Kansas.

The farmhouse was quiet. Daniel had been nothing but a gentleman the night before, showing her to the guest room and explaining that he would sleep in the barn *"until she was more comfortable with the arrangements."*

His kindness had both relieved and touched her, though she suspected the neighbors might think it odd for a newly married husband to sleep in the barn.

Grace rose and dressed quickly, her stomach churning with nerves. She could hear Daniel moving around outside, doing morning chores.

As his wife, she would be expected to have breakfast ready when he came in. The thought filled her with dread.

She made her way to the kitchen, a cheerful room with blue gingham curtains and a large cast-iron stove that dominated one wall.

Grace stared at the stove as if it were a sleeping dragon. At home, she had watched Cook prepare simple meals, but she had never actually operated a stove herself.

"How hard can it be?" she murmured, rolling up her sleeves.

Grace found eggs in the pantry, along with bacon wrapped in brown paper and what appeared to be flour for biscuits. She had watched Cook make biscuits dozens of times—surely she could manage something so basic.

The stove, however, proved to be her first adversary. Grace opened various doors and compartments, trying to understand how to make it produce heat.

She found kindling and matches, but her first attempt at lighting a fire produced more smoke than flame.

On her third try, she got a fire going, though smoke continued to billow out around the edges of the stove door.

"The damper," she realized, remembering something Cook had mentioned. Grace fumbled with various knobs and levers until the smoke finally began drawing up the chimney instead of filling the room.

Feeling triumphant, she set a large iron skillet on the stove and began laying strips of bacon in it. The bacon started cooking a bit too quickly.

Grace turned her attention to the biscuits, mixing flour with what she hoped was the right amount of milk and... something else. Salt? Or was it sugar? She added a generous amount of white granules from a nearby canister.

Behind her, the bacon sizzled loudly. Grace glanced back to see grease popping and splattering.

She grabbed a wooden spoon to turn the strips, but they were cooking much faster than she expected. The edges were already turning dark.

With panic setting in, Grace tried to manage both the bacon and the biscuit dough.

She rolled the dough out on the wooden counter, but it seemed too sticky. She added more flour, and then more milk when it became too dry. The result was a gray, lumpy mass that bore little resemblance to Cook's smooth, white biscuit dough.

The smell of burning bacon filled the kitchen. Grace rushed back to the stove, but the strips were now black on one side and still raw on the other. She tried to flip them, but they crumbled into charred pieces.

Fighting back tears of frustration, Grace pressed on.

She cut the biscuit dough into uneven rounds and placed

them on a baking sheet, sliding it into the oven portion of the stove.

Then she cracked eggs into the bacon grease, but the pan was so hot that the egg whites turned brown and crispy around the edges while the yolks remained raw.

The kitchen door opened just as smoke began pouring from the oven.

"Grace?" Daniel's voice carried concern and a hint of alarm. "Is everything all right?"

Grace spun around, her face flushed with heat and embarrassment, her hair escaping from its pins, and her apron stained with grease.

"I... the biscuits are burning!"

Daniel rushed to the stove, grabbing a thick towel to pull the biscuit pan from the oven.

The bread was black on the bottom and pale gray on top, with an odd, yeasty smell that suggested something had gone very wrong with the recipe.

"Oh no," Grace whispered, staring at the disaster spread across the kitchen.

The bacon was charcoal, the eggs were rubber, and the biscuits looked like stones. "I've ruined everything."

Daniel set the charred biscuits on the counter and turned to survey the damage.

His expression was unreadable as he took in the smoking pan, the scattered flour, and Grace's obvious distress.

"I'm so sorry," Grace said, her voice breaking. "I know you expected a wife who could cook and keep house, but I... I ...we had a cook, we had servants, and I never ..."

She stopped, realizing she was revealing more about her privileged background than she intended.

Daniel was quiet for a long moment, and Grace braced

herself for his anger. After all, Uncle had paid him to take her, and now he was discovering just what a poor bargain he had made.

Instead, Daniel walked to the window and opened it, waving away the smoke. Then he turned back to Grace with the beginning of a smile.

"Well," he said, "I reckon we won't starve. Mrs. Clarkson sent over a sugar pie, a loaf of bread, and a small ham yesterday, and there's butter and jam in the pantry. We can make do until..." He paused, studying her face. "Until you're ready to try again."

Grace stared at him in amazement. "You're not angry?"

"Angry?" Daniel's surprise was genuine. "Grace, you arrived yesterday after traveling hundreds of miles to marry a stranger. Today you got up at dawn to make me breakfast in a kitchen you'd never seen before. Why would I be angry?"

"Because I'm supposed to be a proper farm wife, and I can't even cook eggs without burning them." Grace's voice was small and defeated.

Daniel stepped closer, careful not to crowd her. "Grace, did you think I expected you to know everything on your first day? Marriage is about learning new things, isn't it?"

Grace felt tears prick her eyes. His kindness was almost harder to bear than anger would have been.

How could she tell him it was true when Uncle painted her as a burden, as someone who would require payment to take? How could she explain she felt like a fraud who had tricked him into marriage?

"Come on," Daniel said gently, taking the ruined pan from her hands. "Let's clean this up together, and then I'll show you how to work the stove. Mrs. Clarkson offered to come by this week to help you get settled. I think we should take her up on that offer."

As Grace nodded gratefully, she couldn't help but wonder: if Daniel was being paid to endure her presence, why was he being so patient?

The question gnawed at her as they worked side by side to clean the kitchen, and she found herself more confused than ever about the true nature of their arrangement.

CHAPTER 7

Three days after the breakfast disaster, Daniel appeared at the kitchen door as Grace was attempting to make coffee without burning it.

She managed to get the stove to light properly this time, though the coffee still tasted stronger than boiled tree bark.

"Grace," Daniel stood, hat in hand, "I was wondering if you'd like to come help with the morning milking. Pearl's getting used to having you around, and I thought you might want to learn."

Grace looked up from her cup of bitter coffee, surprised by the invitation. "You want me to milk the cow?"

"Well, it's one of the daily chores that has to be done, and if something ever happened to me, you need to know how."

Daniel's practical tone made sense, but Grace felt her stomach tighten with nerves.

"Besides, it's not that difficult once you get the hang of it."

Grace set down her coffee cup and smoothed her skirts. How hard could it be? She had watched dairymaids from the carriage window back home. They made it look simple enough.

"All right," she said, trying to sound confident. "I'd like to learn."

The barn was warm and filled with the sweet smell of hay. Pearl, a large brown and white cow, stood placidly in her stall. She chewed, regarding Grace with large, patient eyes.

"She's... a bit bigger than I expected," Grace stood carefully behind Daniel.

Daniel chuckled. "Pearl's gentle as a lamb. Aren't you, girl?" He patted the cow's flank affectionately. "She's been with me for five years now, never given me a day of trouble."

He positioned a three-legged stool beside the cow and set a clean milk pail underneath her belly. "The key is to be confident but gentle. Pearl can sense if you're nervous, and it makes her nervous too."

Grace nodded, though she was already feeling nervous enough for both of them.

"Sit down here," Daniel guided Grace to the stool. "Now, you want to use your thumb and forefinger to pinch off the milk at the top, then squeeze with the rest of your fingers to push it down. Like this."

Daniel demonstrated, and streams of warm milk hit the bottom of the pail with a steady rhythm. It looked effortless.

"See? Just like that. Your turn."

Grace settled herself on the stool, acutely aware of how large Pearl was, and she was right beside her. She tentatively reached out and grasped the cow's udder, trying to remember Daniel's instructions.

"Don't be afraid to take hold," Daniel encouraged. "She won't bite."

Grace tightened her grip and attempted the pinching motion Daniel had shown her. Nothing happened. She tried again, squeezing harder.

"Gentle but firm," Daniel coached. "You're being too timid."

Grace squeezed again, and this time milk spurted out—but instead of going into the pail, it shot sideways, splattering against the barn wall.

"Almost," Daniel said patiently. "Do that again, just aim it toward the bucket."

Grace adjusted her position and tried again. This time the milk went in roughly the right direction, though most of it hit the rim of the pail and splashed onto her skirt.

"I'm getting milk everywhere except where it's supposed to go," Grace said, frustration creeping into her voice.

"It takes practice," Daniel assured her. "Try using both hands and alternate between them."

Grace attempted to establish a rhythm like she had seen Daniel use. For a moment, it seemed to work—thin streams of milk made it into the pail. Encouraged, Grace squeezed harder and faster.

That's when Pearl decided she'd had enough.

The cow shifted sideways, bumping against Grace just as she was squeezing. The motion threw off Grace's balance and her aim. Milk sprayed in a wide arc, hitting Daniel in the chest and splashing across his face.

"Oh!" Grace gasped, jerking backward in surprise.

Her sudden movement startled Pearl, who stepped sideways again—right on top of the milk pail. The pail toppled, sending what little milk Grace had collected splashing across the barn floor.

However, the cow wasn't done. Deciding that this milking session was over, Pearl swished her tail hard—right across Grace's face, leaving her sputtering and covered in cow hair.

Grace scrambled off the stool so fast she knocked it over, stumbled backward, and sat down hard in a pile of hay, her skirts flying up above her knees.

For a moment, the barn was silent except for Pearl's swishing tail and Grace's heavy breathing.

Grace looked up to see Daniel standing very still, milk dripping from his hair, down his face, and soaking the front of his shirt. His expression was blank.

"I'm sorry," Grace whispered, scrambling to her feet and brushing hay from her skirt. "I'm so sorry, Daniel. I don't know what happened. She just moved, and I—"

"It's all right," Daniel said, though his voice sounded strained. He pulled out a handkerchief and began wiping milk from his face. "Accidents happen."

Grace watched him clean himself off, noting the tight set of his jaw and the way he was deliberately not looking at her.

"You're angry."

"I'm not angry," Daniel said, but he righted the overturned pail with more force than necessary.

"You are. I can tell." Grace twisted her hands in her skirt. "I've ruined everything again. First breakfast, now this. I'm useless."

Daniel stopped wiping his face and looked at her then, taking in her hay-covered appearance and distressed expression. Some of the tension went out of his shoulders.

"Grace, you're not useless. You're just...learning."

"Learning to be a disaster." Grace's voice was miserable. "Your cousin's wife was right—you planted flowers because you hoped I'd be someone who deserved them. But I'm not. I can't cook, I can't milk a cow, and I probably can't do anything useful on a farm."

Daniel was quiet for a moment, studying her face. "Grace, why do you keep talking like you're some kind of burden I'm stuck with?"

Grace felt heat creep up her neck. She couldn't very well tell him she knew about Uncle's payment, not when she was already proving to be such a poor bargain.

"I know this isn't what you expected when you agreed to marry me."

Daniel set down his handkerchief and stepped closer. "Grace, just what do you think I expected?"

Before Grace could answer, Pearl mooed loudly, as if reminding them she still needed to be milked.

Daniel glanced at the cow, then back at Grace. "We'll finish this conversation later. For now, why don't you go get cleaned up? I'll take care of milking Pearl."

Grace nodded, grateful for the escape, though she could feel Daniel's puzzled gaze following her as she hurried from the barn.

She was making such a mess of everything, and she couldn't understand why he was still being so patient with her.

If only she knew whether his kindness came from genuine care or from the duty of a man paid to endure her presence.

CHAPTER 8

First thing the next morning, Mrs. Clarkson arrived at the Carrington farm with a large wicker basket, a box, and a determined smile.

Grace watched from the kitchen window as the older woman climbed down from a wagon, her gray hair neatly hidden beneath a white bonnet.

"Good morning, dear!" Mrs. Clarkson called out as Grace opened the door. "I thought it was time we had a proper cooking lesson. Daniel mentioned you might appreciate some instruction in the kitchen."

Grace felt her cheeks burn with embarrassment. "I'm afraid I'm quite hopeless. You're very kind to offer, but I don't want to waste your time."

"Nonsense!" Mrs. Clarkson bustled into the kitchen, setting her basket on the wooden table. "Every woman can learn to cook; it just takes patience and practice. Now, I've brought some supplies, and we're going to start with the basics. Biscuits, a simple pie, and maybe some stew for dinner."

Mrs. Clarkson moved around the kitchen with the assurance of someone who had been cooking for decades. She examined Grace's flour and supplies, making small approving sounds.

"First thing," she said, rolling up her sleeves, "is understanding your ingredients. This here is your flour—hold out your hand. Feel how fine it is? And this," she picked up the canister Grace had used in her attempt to make biscuits, "is salt. Sugar's in the blue tin over there. It's not hard to make a mistake and mix them up."

Grace winced. "So that's why the biscuits tasted so strange."

"Could have been worse! Could have been baking soda!" Mrs. Clarkson's laugh was loud. "Now, biscuits are all about the touch. Light hands, cold lard or butter, and don't overwork the dough."

As they worked together, Mrs. Clarkson's gentle instructions began to make sense.

The older woman showed Grace how to cut the lard into the flour until it resembled coarse crumbs, how to make a well for the milk, and how to fold the dough just until it came together.

"You're getting it," Mrs. Clarkson encouraged as Grace carefully cut out the biscuits. "Much better than my first attempt. I put so much salt in mine that my poor husband couldn't eat them because of the bitter taste."

"I'm sure your husband was more understanding than mine will be," Grace said quietly, placing the biscuits on the baking sheet. "Daniel married me sight unseen, after all. I have no doubt he expected someone who knew how to keep house."

Mrs. Clarkson paused in her measuring of the pie ingredients. "Grace, dear, what exactly did your family tell you about this marriage arrangement?"

Grace felt heat filling her face. She busied herself with cleaning the counter. "My uncle handled everything. He said...he said Daniel required a dowry to take on someone like me. A woman with no actual skills and expensive tastes."

"A dowry?" Mrs. Clarkson's voice was sharp with surprise. "Child, what on earth do you mean?"

"Uncle had to pay him." Grace could not meet the older woman's eyes. "He got paid three hundred dollars to marry me. I know I'm not much of a bargain. I can't cook, I've never done real housework, and I come with nothing but debts. Uncle made it clear that no man would ever want me for myself."

Mrs. Clarkson was silent for a long moment, and Grace could feel her stare. Her voice was controlled when she spoke. "Grace, who told you that Daniel was paid to marry you?"

"My uncle. He arranged everything after Father died. He said the only way to find me a husband was to pay someone willing to take on such a burden."

"And you believed him?"

Grace finally looked up, surprised by the odd tone in Mrs. Clarkson's voice. "Why would he lie about such a thing?"

Mrs. Clarkson opened her mouth to say something, then seemed to think better of it. She turned back to the pie filling, her movements more brisk than before.

"Well, with families, sometimes the truth isn't what it seems."

As they worked on the pie crust—Mrs. Clarkson guided Grace's hands as she rolled the dough—the older woman spoke, her tone firm.

"Daniel's a good man, Grace. One of the best I know. After what happened with Priscilla, I thought he might never marry at all."

Grace's hands stilled on the rolling pin. "Priscilla?"

"His former fiancée. They were engaged for close to two years." Mrs. Clarkson's voice carried a note of old anger. "Beautiful girl, but restless. She decided farm life wasn't exciting enough for her and ran off to Kansas City with a traveling salesman just three months before their wedding."

Grace felt something twist in her stomach. "How terrible for him."

"Broke his heart, it did. He threw himself into the farm work after that and hardly spoke to anyone for months. When he started talking about finding a wife, he said he wanted someone who would appreciate a simple life, someone looking for a real home rather than adventure."

Mrs. Clarkson glanced at Grace. "He said he'd rather marry someone who chose him deliberately, through correspondence, than risk his heart on someone local who might change her mind."

Grace stared down at the pie crust, her mind reeling. This didn't sound like a man who had been paid to take an unwanted burden. This sounded like a man who was hurt and was trying to find a woman to value what he offered.

"He made the choice to find a mail-order bride?"

"Chose it, planned it, and was as nervous as a schoolboy waiting for your answer to his first letter." Mrs. Clarkson's smile was soft. "I've never seen him happier than he was this past month, getting the house ready for you."

As they slid the pie into the oven, Grace struggled with the conflicting information.

"Mrs. Clarkson, if Daniel wanted a wife, why would my uncle need to pay him anything?"

The older woman turned to face Grace, her expression troubled.

"Grace, dear, I think there may be some confusion about this bride arrangement. Daniel never mentioned receiving any money. In fact, he sent money to your uncle for your train ticket, and he's been spending his own savings to fix up the house and buy things he thought you might like."

Grace felt the blood drain from her face. "That can't be right. Uncle was very clear about the payment."

"Perhaps," Mrs. Clarkson said gently, "your uncle didn't completely disclose what was really arranged."

The words hung in the air between them like smoke from a poorly tended fire. Grace sank onto a kitchen chair, her mind spinning.

If Uncle had lied about the dowry, what else had he lied about? And if Daniel hadn't been paid to take her, what did that mean about their marriage?

"I don't understand," Grace whispered. "Why would Uncle lie?"

Mrs. Clarkson sat down across the table, reaching over to pat Grace's hand.

"I don't know, dear. But I do know this: Daniel Carrington is not a man who would marry for money. He's been alone by choice for over three years because he was waiting for the right woman. If he chose you, it's because he wanted you, not because he was paid to take you."

Grace felt tears prick her eyes. Since she had arrived at the farm, she had been waiting for Daniel to show his true feelings about being stuck with an unwanted burden. Instead, his actions were gentle, understanding, and thoughtful, as if he truly valued her company.

"What should I do?" Grace asked.

"For now? Learn to make a proper biscuit and try to get to know your husband. And maybe...maybe ask him about the arrangement yourself. Men aren't mind readers, Grace. If you've been holding back because you think he doesn't want you, he might be thinking you don't want him."

As the smell of baking apples filled the kitchen, Grace realized that her uncle's lies had been poisoning her marriage from the very beginning.

The question now was whether it was too late to start over with the truth.

CHAPTER 9

Daniel stepped through the kitchen door as the sun was setting, taking in the sight before him: the table set with their best dishes, a pot of fragrant stew simmering on the stove, and a golden-brown pie cooling on the windowsill.

"Something smells wonderful," he said, hanging his hat on the peg by the door.

Grace turned from the stove, her face flushed with heat and excitement, wisps of hair escaping from their pins. But unlike the morning disasters, this flush came from triumph rather than embarrassment.

"Mrs. Clarkson taught me to make beef stew today. And biscuits that aren't burned. And we made an apple pie for dessert."

There was something different in her voice—a note of genuine pride that Daniel hadn't heard before.

Grace ladled the stew into bowls, her movements careful but confident.

"Here," she said, setting a bowl before him with a shy smile. "Try it. Mrs. Clarkson said the secret is browning the meat first and adding the vegetables at just the right time so they don't get mushy."

Daniel took a spoonful and raised his eyebrows in surprise. The stew was rich and flavorful, the meat tender, and the vegetables perfectly cooked.

"Grace, this is delicious."

Her face lit up like the sunrise. "Really? You're not just being nice?"

"I'm being honest. This is better than anything I've eaten in months." Daniel took another bite, watching Grace glow with pleasure at his praise.

She settled across from him, breaking open a biscuit of her own. It was light and fluffy, and Grace realized she was starving.

"Mrs. Clarkson said stew is one of the easiest things to make once you understand the principles. You just have to be patient and let it cook slowly." Grace stirred her stew for a minute. "She said I was a quick learner."

As they ate, Grace relaxed in a way Daniel hadn't seen before. The anxious tension that usually held her shoulders rigid seemed to melt away, replaced by something warm and genuine.

"You know," Grace said, spreading butter on her biscuit, "Mrs. Clarkson told me about the schoolteacher, Miss Crawford. She might need help with the younger children."

Grace looked at Daniel. "I was thinking...if you wouldn't mind...I might offer to help her. I'm good with letters and numbers, and I love children."

Daniel paused with his spoon halfway to his mouth. "Of course I wouldn't mind. I think that's a wonderful idea."

Grace's eyes sparkled. "I taught my neighbor's little girl to read back home. She was only five, but so bright. We would sit in the garden and sound out words together."

Grace's smile was soft with memory. "Her mother said she'd seen no one have such patience with children."

Watching her face as she spoke, Daniel felt something shift in his chest. This was the first time Grace had mentioned anything specific about her life before Prescott, and when she talked about teaching, her whole being seemed to come alive.

"Tell me more about home, and about your life there."

Grace's spoon paused halfway to her mouth, and some of the light dimmed in her eyes.

"There's not much worth telling. Father died suddenly, and...well, everything in the world changed after that." But then she seemed to shake off the shadow of the memories.

"Oh! Mrs. Clarkson showed me how to make apple jelly today, too! When the apple harvest comes in, we can put up dozens of jars of apple preserves for the winter. And she's going to teach me to make soap next week."

Grace leaned forward, her eyes shining. "I never realized how much there was to learn about keeping a proper house."

Daniel found himself captivated by this animated version of his new wife. Without her usual tension, Grace was wonderful, clever, and incredibly amusing.

"Mrs. Clarkson told me about your chickens," Grace said, cutting into her pie with obvious pride. "You've been wanting to expand the flock, and I could help with that. I'm not afraid of chickens."

She paused, then added with a rueful laugh, "Though I might be afraid of everything else on the farm."

"You're doing better than you think." Daniel's praise was honest. "And Grace...you don't have to prove anything to me."

The words seemed to hit her like a physical blow. Grace's fork clattered to her plate, and the brightness faded from her face.

"Don't I?"

"What do you mean?"

Grace looked down at her hands. "I just...I know I'm not what you expected. I can't cook, well, I couldn't cook, but now I can cook a little. I know nothing about farm life, and I come with nothing but..."

She stopped abruptly, as if catching herself before saying too much.

Daniel set down his spoon and leaned forward. "Grace, look at me."

She raised her eyes.

"You keep saying you're not what I expected, but you've never asked me what I did expect. Or why I wanted a wife in the first place."

Grace's throat worked as if she was struggling to swallow.

"Because you needed help with the farm?"

"Partly," Daniel admitted. "But mostly because I was lonely. I want a partner, Grace. Someone to share this life with. Someone to talk to over supper, someone to plan for the future with."

He gestured around the cozy kitchen. "Someone who could make this house feel like a home."

Grace's eyes filled with tears, and Daniel felt a stab of concern. His words should have comforted her, but she looked stricken.

"What is it?" he asked gently. "What's troubling you?"

Grace opened her mouth as if to speak, then closed it again. She looked around the kitchen at the successful meal, the warm lamplight, the evidence of her ability to learn quickly. Daniel could see her wrestling with something.

"I want to be a good wife to you," she whispered. "I want to deserve this chance."

"Deserve it?" Daniel's brow furrowed. "Grace, what do you mean? You're my wife. You don't have to earn your place here."

But Grace had already risen from the table, beginning to clear the dishes with quick, nervous movements.

"Would you like more pie?" she asked, her voice artificially bright. "There's plenty left."

Daniel watched her bustle around the kitchen, noting how she avoided his eyes. Something was weighing on his wife, something that made her feel she had to prove her worth instead of accepting that she belonged here.

He didn't know what burden she was carrying, but he was realizing it was larger than just learning to cook and manage a household.

As Grace served him another slice of perfect apple pie, Daniel made a silent promise to himself. Whatever was troubling his wife, whatever had put that shadow in her eyes, he would help her past it.

Because the woman he had glimpsed tonight, bright, eager, full of warmth and intelligence, was the partner he had hoped for when he found a mail-order bride.

Now, he just had to convince her she was wanted, not merely tolerated.

CHAPTER 10

As Grace's culinary triumphs continued to grow, Daniel declared it was time to gather eggs. The morning was crisp and clear, with early falling leaves dancing across the farmyard.

"The chickens are used to you being around now," Daniel said, setting down his coffee cup. "Gathering eggs every morning is important for the health of the flock, and we always need eggs for cooking. Mrs. Clarkson said you're planning to try her cake recipe this week?"

Grace felt a flutter of fear, but also excitement. After her recent kitchen successes, she was eager to take on more farm responsibilities.

"I'd like that. How difficult can it be?"

Daniel's lips twitched to hide a smile. "Famous last words, but it's much easier than milking Pearl. The chickens ignore you if you move slow and don't startle them."

He handed her a wicker basket and led her toward the chicken coop, a neat wooden structure behind the barn.

"Most of the hens lay in nesting boxes, but a few of them

like to hide their eggs in corners or under things. You'll learn their habits."

The chicken yard was alive with activity. A dozen hens pecked and scratched in the dirt, clucking to themselves. A magnificent rooster strutted among them, his red comb gleaming in the morning sun.

"That's Napoleon," Daniel said, pointing to the rooster. "He's protective of his ladies, but he won't bother you if you don't bother him. Just move slow and speak quiet."

Grace watched the chickens with fascination. She had never been this close to farm animals before coming to Prescott, and she found their busy, persistent movements soothing.

"Good morning, ladies," she murmured, stepping into the coop. Several hens looked up at her with bright, curious eyes before returning to the important work of scratching for bugs.

Daniel showed her the row of nesting boxes built along one wall.

"See? Three eggs already this morning."

He showed Grace how to slide her hand under a hen to check for eggs, moving slowly so as not to startle the bird.

"The trick is confidence," he explained. "If you're flustered, they sense it and get agitated. Just be calm and gentle."

Grace nodded, watching as he quickly collected eggs from several boxes. It looked simple enough.

"Your turn." Daniel handed her the basket. "I'll watch from here in case you need help."

Grace approached the nearest nesting box, where a plump red hen sat in silence.

"Hello there, beautiful," she crooned, moving as Daniel had instructed. "I just need to check if you have an egg for me today."

To her delight, the hen seemed unbothered as Grace carefully slid her hand underneath. Her fingers touched something smooth and warm.

"I found one!" Grace was triumphant, lifting out a perfect brown egg.

"Well done!" Grace could hear genuine pride in Daniel's voice. "See? You're a natural."

Encouraged, Grace moved to the next box. The hen eyed Grace warily, her feathers bristling, yet she stayed put. Grace found two more eggs, placing them carefully in her basket.

"This is wonderful." Grace felt her confidence growing. "They're so much calmer than Pearl."

"Don't let that fool you," Daniel laughed. "Chickens can be just as unpredictable. But they're smaller, so the damage usually isn't as bad."

Grace was reaching for an egg in a corner nesting box when she saw something that made her freeze. Coiled in the shadows beneath the roosting perch was a long, thick snake, its scales shiny in the morning light.

For a moment Grace stared, her mind not quite processing what she was seeing. The snake was at least four feet long and as thick as her wrist, its tongue flicking out to taste the air.

"Daniel," Grace said, her voice very calm and very quiet. "There's a snake."

"Where?" Daniel's voice sharpened.

"Under the roosting perch. It's...it's quite large."

Daniel moved quickly until he could see the snake. His expression relaxed. "It's just a rat snake, Grace. They're not dangerous, they're helpful because they eat the rats and mice that would steal the chicken feed."

"It's not dangerous?" Grace asked, still frozen in place.

"Not to you. But it might eat eggs, which is less helpful." Daniel looked around for something to encourage the snake to leave. "They're more afraid of you than you are of them."

Grace looked at the snake again, noting its sleek scales and the graceful way it moved.

"It's quite beautiful," she said, surprising herself. "I've never seen a snake this close before."

Daniel paused in his search for a stick, looking at her with amazement. Most women would have been screaming and running by now.

"You're not afraid?"

"He startled me," Grace admitted, "but he's not trying to hurt anyone. He's just looking for a meal."

She studied the snake. "This one is doing us a favor if he's here to keep the mouse population down."

The snake, deciding the chicken coop had become too crowded for its liking, slithered toward a gap in the floorboards. Grace watched its fluid motion with fascination.

"It's leaving on its own," she observed. "Maybe it just wanted to check if there were any eggs worth taking."

Daniel shook his head in amazement. "Grace, most women would have fainted or run screaming from the coop."

"I've never seen the point in hysterics." Grace smiled, pleased by his admiring look. "Father always said that panic rarely improves any situation. Besides, you said the snake wasn't dangerous."

"Even so, your calm reaction is...remarkable."

Grace glowed at Daniel's praise. For once, her response had been right instead of wrong.

"I think growing up in the city teaches you that most creatures are just trying to live their lives, same as people. The snake wasn't threatening anyone, it was just in the wrong place."

When the snake disappeared, Grace turned back to her egg collecting. She found three more eggs, including one that had rolled into a corner where the snake had been resting.

"I think I rather like the chickens," Grace said as they left the coop, her basket full of fresh eggs. "They seem to each have distinct personalities. And the work is useful and important."

Daniel watched his wife as they walked back to the house, noting the confident set of her shoulders and the satisfaction in her voice.

This was the same woman who had nearly burned down the kitchen making breakfast, yet she had just faced a snake with more composure than most men he knew.

"Grace, you continue to surprise me."

She looked up at him, a smile playing at the corners of her mouth. "In a good way, I hope?"

"In the best way." Daniel studied her face, seeing something he had missed before. There was strength in Grace, actual strength beneath all her anxiety about not being a proper farm wife.

"I think you're going to do just fine here."

Grace's smile faltered, and that familiar shadow crossed her face. "Even though I'm not what you bargained for?"

"Grace." Daniel stopped walking and turned to face her. "I wish you would stop saying things like that. What exactly do you think I bargained for?"

For a moment, it looked as though Grace might answer him. Her mouth opened, and he could see her struggling with something. But then she seemed to catch herself.

"I should get these eggs inside and start on the bread for lunch," she said, deflecting once again. "Mrs. Clarkson said the secret to good cornbread is not to over-mix the batter."

Daniel watched her hurry toward the house, frustration and concern warring in his chest. Every time they seemed to make headway, every time Grace showed him the remarkable woman she was, something pulled her back into that defensive shell he couldn't seem to break.

Whatever burden his wife was carrying, whatever had

convinced her she wasn't wanted or wasn't good enough, it was standing between them like a wall.

Daniel was realizing that until that wall came down, they would never be partners, no matter how many successful meals she cooked or how bravely she faced down snakes.

But today, watching her handle the snake situation with such grace and common sense, he had seen glimpses of the woman Grace could be when she wasn't weighed down by whatever secret shame she carried.

That woman was worth fighting for, and worth the patience it would take to help her find her way back to herself.

As he followed her into the house, Daniel made another silent promise. Somehow, he would show Grace that she was not just tolerated or endured, but wanted and valued.

Whatever it took.

CHAPTER II

Not long after the chicken coop incident, Mrs. Clarkson arrived at the Carrington farm with her wagon hitched and ready.

"Time for your first proper shopping trip to Prescott," she cheerfully announced. "You'll need supplies for seasonal canning, and I thought you should meet some of the other ladies in town."

Grace smoothed her dress, a deep green brocade that had been one of her finer day gowns back East. She climbed up beside Mrs. Clarkson.

Daniel waved goodbye from the barn, calling out, "Don't let her spend all our money, Mrs. Clarkson!"

"As if I would!" Grace laughed back, feeling lighter than she had in weeks. The early autumn air was crisp, the countryside was beautiful, and she was looking forward to seeing more of her new surroundings.

"Now," Mrs. Clarkson explained as they rolled toward town, "we'll stop at the dry goods store for fabric and such, and we'll pick up supplies at the general store. I thought we'd have lunch in the hotel dining room so you can meet some of the other ladies."

The Prescott General Store was bustling with morning activity.

Grace marveled at the variety of goods crammed into the space, everything from farming implements to bolts of fabric to jars of preserves. Mr. Zimmerman, a kindly man with twinkling eyes, greeted Grace warmly.

"So you're Daniel's bride! Welcome to Prescott, Mrs. Carrington. How are you settling in?"

"Very well, thank you," Grace replied. "Oh my, this store looks like the very heart of the town! I can see why things are so busy, you've got anything anyone in town might need."

Mr. Zimmerman was immediately smitten. "If you need any help at all, Mrs. Carrington, please let my wife or me know. She's right over there behind the counter, weighing up sugar for a customer."

As Grace and Mrs. Clarkson moved through the store gathering supplies, Grace found herself drawn to a display of children's slate boards and chalk.

She picked one up and looked it over. Did the local school use something like this? How well equipped was the school with supplies?

"Planning ahead, are we?" came a sharp voice behind her.

Grace turned to see a thin woman with steel-gray hair and calculating eyes. The woman was well-dressed but in a severe, disapproving way that made Grace feel self-conscious.

"Oh, hello," Grace was polite. "I don't believe we've met. I'm Grace Carrington. "

"Mrs. Agnes Whiteman," the woman replied, her tone cool. "I heard Daniel Carrington had taken a mail-order bride. From back East, I'm told."

"Yes, I'm from Massachusetts." Grace set the slate board

back on the counter, feeling as though she had been caught doing something inappropriate.

"And you're looking at children's school supplies already?" Mrs. Whiteman's eyebrows rose into her hairline. "My, my. That was...quick."

Grace blushed, suddenly understanding the implication. "Oh no, I was just thinking about the local school. Mrs. Clarkson mentioned that Miss Crawford might need help with the younger children. I used to teach back home."

But Mrs. Whiteman's expression had already shifted to one of thinly concealed disapproval.

"I see. Well, I suppose someone will need to help those poor children if Miss Crawford takes ill again." With that, Agnes Whiteman turned on her heel and marched off.

Grace stared at the woman's retreating back, gripped by a growing sense of unease.

~

NEXT DOOR, at the dry goods store, Grace found a bolt of fine blue silk that reminded her of a dress her mother had once owned. She ran her fingers over the smooth material, lost in memory.

"Beautiful, isn't it?" Mrs. Clarkson ran her hand down the roll. "So soft, but perhaps a bit fine for everyday farm wear."

"Oh, I wasn't thinking of buying it," Grace said quickly. "It just reminded me of something my mother once wore. She would have loved the color."

Unfortunately, Agnes Whiteman had followed them into the shop and overheard.

"Your mother had silk dresses? How.. interesting. I wouldn't have thought Massachusetts farmers could afford such luxuries."

Grace felt her face flush. "My father wasn't a farmer. He was in business."

"Business?" Mrs. Whiteman's eyes sharpened. "What kind of business?"

"Banking and investments," Grace replied, wishing she could take the words back as soon as she said them. She was revealing too much about her background to a complete stranger.

Mrs. Whiteman's smile was thin and knowing. "Ah. A banker's daughter. That explains quite a lot, doesn't it?"

Twice in one day Grace found herself staring at the woman's retreating back. That feeling of unease gripping Grace was now tinged with fear.

LUNCH at the Cozart Hotel should have been pleasant. Mrs. Clarkson introduced Grace to several other ladies from town: the banker's wife, the doctor's wife, the local dress shop owner, the wife of the Baptist minister, and two farmers' wives who were genuine with their welcome.

The conversation was light and friendly, covering topics from the upcoming fall harvest festival to their winter food preparations.

Grace was beginning to relax when Agnes Whiteman arrived with two other women and seated herself at a nearby table, within easy earshot.

"I don't know why Daniel Carrington needed to send all the way to Massachusetts for a wife," Mrs. Whiteman said in a voice clearly meant to carry. "Plenty of good local girls would have been happy to marry him."

Grace felt her cheeks burn, and Mrs. Clarkson squeezed her hand under the table in support.

"Some men prefer a fresh start," Mrs. Clarkson said diplomatically.

"A fresh start, perhaps," Mrs. Whiteman continued, "but I wonder what kind of fresh start requires a banker's daughter to flee all the way to Prescott, Kansas? She's already shopping for children's school supplies, I noticed. One does wonder about the...urgency...of the arrangement."

The other ladies at Grace's table looked uncomfortable, and Grace felt as though she had been slapped.

The implication was clear—Mrs. Whiteman was suggesting Grace had gotten into some kind of trouble that required a hasty marriage and quick escape from her home in Boston.

"I think," said Mrs. Margaret Kildare, the doctor's wife, "that some people have altogether too much interest in other people's private affairs."

But the damage was done. Grace could see the speculation in several pairs of eyes, and she knew there would be whispered conversations that would follow.

LATER THAT AFTERNOON, as Grace and Mrs. Clarkson loaded the last of their purchases into the wagon, Reverend Shoemaker approached them on the sidewalk. His kind face radiated genuine warmth as he tipped his hat.

"Mrs. Carrington! How lovely to see you again. I trust you're settling in well?"

"Very well, thank you, Reverend," Grace replied, though she could feel Mrs. Whiteman's penetrating gaze from across the street.

"Wonderful to hear. I do hope we'll see you and Daniel at services Sunday morning. The congregation is eager to welcome you properly to our community."

His smile was so sincere that Grace felt some of her tension ease.

"That's very kind. I'll speak with Daniel about it."

"Excellent! Services begin at ten o'clock. And Mrs. Carrington," he added gently, "please know that our church is a place of welcome for all God's children. I hope you'll find it a comfort."

Grace nodded, touched by his words, though she couldn't shake the feeling that Mrs. Whiteman had somehow heard every word despite being across the street.

The journey back to the farm was quiet. Mrs. Clarkson finally broke the silence as they turned onto the Carrington property.

"Don't you mind Agnes Whiteman, dear. She's been stirring up trouble in this town for too many years. Most folks know to take anything she says with a grain of salt."

"But some people will believe her," Grace whispered. "She made it sound like I'm some kind of fallen woman who had to flee Massachusetts in disgrace."

"Anyone with eyes in their head can see you're a lady, Grace. Your manners, your speech, the way you carry yourself—it's obvious you come from a good family."

"That's almost worse," Grace murmured. "If I come from such a good family, why would I need to marry a complete stranger and travel halfway across the country? What must people think?"

Mrs. Clarkson was quiet for a moment. "Grace, is there something about your situation that you haven't told me? Some reason you felt you had to leave home?"

Grace stared down at her hands, thinking of Uncle's cruelty, the stolen jewelry, the possible lies about the dowry.

How could she explain she hadn't chosen to leave, but that she'd been sold like livestock to the highest bidder?

"My father died and left debts," she admitted. "My uncle came in and sold everything we owned to pay that debt. It was my uncle who arranged the marriage. It seemed like an arranged marriage was the best option available to me."

It was true, even if it wasn't the whole truth. Mrs. Clarkson nodded in sympathy.

"Many women have found themselves in similar circumstances, dear. There's no shame in making the best of a difficult time. But perhaps..." she hesitated. "Perhaps it would be wise not to mention your father's business too much. Some folks might not understand that losing everything can happen to anyone."

As they pulled up to the farmhouse, Grace saw Daniel emerge from the barn, his face lighting up when he saw her. For a moment, her heart lifted. Whatever problems waited in town, at least she had found some sort of happiness here with him.

But Mrs. Whiteman's venomous words echoed in her mind. If the gossip spread, would it reach Daniel? Would he wonder what kind of woman he had married?

Did the rumors have a chance of damaging his reputation, and if that happened, would he think even worse of her than the townspeople already did?

Grace climbed down from the wagon with a heavy heart, realizing that her troubles were far from over.

In fact, they might just be beginning.

CHAPTER 12

Sunday morning Grace dressed carefully in one of her best dresses, a navy blue wool accented with mother-of-pearl buttons and a modest white collar that she hoped would strike the right note of respectability.

Daniel had readily agreed to attend Sunday church services, though he seemed more interested in making Grace happy than in his own spiritual needs.

"You look lovely," he said as he helped her into the wagon. "Though I have to admit, I'm curious to see how the town receives us as a married couple."

Grace's stomach tightened. If he only knew what was already being whispered about her in town.

The ride to town was pleasant, with Daniel pointing out various landmarks and sharing stories about the families of the farms they passed.

Grace tried to focus on his conversation, but her mind kept drifting to Mrs. Whiteman's sharp eyes and sharper tongue.

They arrived at the church with ten minutes to spare, tying their wagon among the others outside the small white building.

Grace saw several familiar faces from her trip to town, including Mrs. Kildare, who nodded kindly in their direction.

As they started to approach the front steps, Daniel paused to adjust the wagon's tie rope. Grace continued forward, but stopped short when she heard voices from around the corner of the building.

Mrs. Whiteman's unmistakable tone carried clearly in the crisp morning air.

"...rushed marriage if I ever saw one. Mark my words, there'll be a baby within six months of her arrival. Why else would a banker's daughter run away to marry a farmer she'd never met?"

"But Agnes," came another woman's voice, "perhaps she simply wanted a different life..."

"Oh, my dear naïve woman," Mrs. Whiteman interrupted with a harsh laugh. "Rich girls don't give up silk dresses and servants to milk cows unless they have to. Something drove her away from Boston, and I'd wager it wasn't a sudden love of farm life."

Grace felt the blood drain from her face. Behind her, she heard Daniel's footsteps stop abruptly—he had clearly heard every word. Wordlessly, he gripped her arm and hurried them both toward the church doors.

Inside the church, Grace tried to focus on Reverend Shoemaker's sermon about forgiveness and Christian charity, but she was acutely aware of the sideways glances from several pews.

Mrs. Whiteman sat prominently in the third row, occasionally turning to murmur something to the woman sitting beside her while looking pointedly in Grace's direction.

Daniel sat rigidly beside her, his jaw set in a way Grace had never seen before. When it came time to greet their neighbors during the service, several people were warm and welcoming, but others offered only polite nods or avoided contact altogether.

Mrs. Kildare made a point of seeking them out after the service. "Grace, dear, I do hope you'll join our ladies' auxiliary. We meet every Thursday to work on quilts for families in need."

"That sounds wonderful," Grace replied gratefully, though she noticed how some of the women standing close to her suddenly found urgent conversations elsewhere when Mrs. Kildare made the invitation.

As they walked back to their wagon, Grace could feel Daniel's silence like a physical weight. He helped her up to the seat with his usual courtesy, but his movements were sharp, almost angry.

They had traveled nearly half the distance home before Daniel spoke, his voice tight with controlled emotion.

"So. Is there something you'd like to tell me about your reasons for leaving Massachusetts?"

Grace's heart pounded. "What do you mean?"

"I mean," Daniel said, still not looking at her, "that apparently half the town thinks you're either with child or running from some scandal. And judging by their certainty, they seem to know something I don't."

"Daniel, it's not what you think—"

"What I think," he interrupted, his voice harder than she'd ever heard it, "is that my wife has been less than honest with me about her circumstances. What I think is that I married a woman who let me believe she was seeking a new life when she was actually fleeing her old one."

Grace felt tears fill her eyes. "That's not fair. I never lied to you."

"Didn't you?" Daniel looked at her, and the hurt and anger on his face shocked Grace. "You've been acting like you're afraid of me, like you're walking on eggshells, like you expect me to throw you out at any moment. Now I'm wondering if that's because you know you deceived me."

"I haven't deceived you!" Grace's voice rose with desperation. "Daniel, if you would just listen—"

"Listen to what? More half-truths? More of you telling me how you're 'not what I expected' and how you don't 'deserve' to be here?" Daniel's hands tightened on the reins. "Maybe you should have been honest from the beginning about whatever it is you're running from."

Grace stared at him, her heart breaking. How could she explain she wasn't running from scandal, but from a cruel uncle who had sold her like livestock? How could she tell him about the dowry without revealing that she knew his secret, that he had been paid to take her?

"Maybe," Daniel continued, his voice bitter, "we should have stayed home today, anyway. I have work that won't wait, and apparently taking my wife to church did nothing but entertain the town gossips."

The words hit Grace like a slap. He was already regretting bringing her, regretting their marriage, regretting the time he'd wasted on her.

"I'm sorry," she whispered, tears now flowing freely. "I never wanted to bring shame to you."

Daniel's expression softened at her tears, but the damage was done.

"Grace, I just...I need to understand what's happening here. These people are talking about you, about our marriage, and I don't know how to defend you because I don't know what I'm defending you from."

The rest of the ride passed in painful silence. Grace stared at her hands, twisted in her lap, while Daniel focused on the road ahead.

The happiness she had found in their growing relationship

now felt fragile and false, threatened by gossip, misunderstandings, and the terrible weight of Uncle's lies.

As they pulled into their farmyard, Grace realized that Mrs. Whiteman had accomplished what she intended. The vile woman had planted seeds of doubt that were already beginning to sprout.

Grace did not know how to stop them from growing into something that would destroy her marriage.

CHAPTER 13

The sound of the kitchen door slamming woke Grace. She had overslept, something she hadn't done since arriving at the farm.

By the time she dressed and hurried downstairs, Daniel was already gone. Only the lingering scent of coffee and the sight of a dirty plate on the counter told her he had been there at all.

She found his coffee cup in the washbasin, along with a fork. He had made his own breakfast rather than wake her. That realization stung more than it should have.

Grace set about preparing a proper breakfast anyway. She fried bacon and eggs, and the biscuits that morning were golden and light.

She kept the food warm on the stove, glancing out the window every few minutes to watch for Daniel's return from the morning chores.

When he finally came in, his boots heavy on the kitchen floor, she served him with a bright smile that felt like glass.

"Good morning," she said, setting the full plate before him. "I'm sorry I overslept. I've made your favorites."

"Thank you," Daniel replied, his voice carefully polite. He

ate in silence, his eyes focused on his plate, and Grace chattered to fill the void.

"Mrs. Clarkson said she'd show me how to make apple butter this week. The trees are heavy with fruit, and it would be a shame to see it go to waste. And I thought I would ask about getting hens started on brooding for spring chicks..."

Daniel nodded at intervals, but Grace could feel the distance between them like a physical wall. When he finished eating, he carried his plate to the washbasin himself.

"I'll be working on the south fence today," he said, not meeting her eyes. "Won't be back until supper."

And then he was gone, leaving Grace alone in the kitchen that suddenly felt too quiet.

Grace threw herself into her domestic duties with conviction. Her actions would show him that she was a good wife and worth keeping.

With military precision, she scrubbed the kitchen floor, polished surfaces, and organized the pantry.

She baked bread and two pies, and prepared a roast that would feed them for days. She even attempted Mrs. Clarkson's complicated apple jelly recipe.

When Daniel came in for supper, the house shone like polished silver and smelled of fresh bread and cinnamon. Grace served him at the dining table with their best china, as if they were entertaining company.

"This is quite a spread," Daniel said, and Grace's heart leapt at what sounded like approval.

"I wanted to try the apple jelly recipe. Mrs. Clarkson said it was your mother's favorite." Grace watched his face hopefully.

Daniel's expression softened slightly. "She would have liked that you're learning her recipes."

But even this small breakthrough faded as the meal progressed in silence. Daniel complimented the food, but his response was brief, polite, and distant. When he left to return to the barn, Grace felt more discouraged than ever.

By Wednesday, Grace had cleaned everything twice. She reorganized the linen closet, mended every piece of clothing that had even the smallest hole, and scrubbed the front porch until the wood changed color.

She picked the last of the garden vegetables and spent hours canning them in neat rows of glass jars.

Mrs. Clarkson stopped by that afternoon and found Grace on her hands and knees, scrubbing the already-clean kitchen floor.

"Goodness, child, what are you doing? This floor is clean enough to eat off of already."

Grace sat back on her heels, pushing a strand of hair from her face. "I just want to make sure everything is perfect."

Mrs. Clarkson's expression grew concerned. "Grace, is everything all right between you and Daniel? You look exhausted."

"Everything's fine," Grace said quickly, forcing another bright smile. "I'm just trying to keep busy. Daniel's been working so hard lately."

But Mrs. Clarkson's knowing look told Grace she wasn't fooled.

When Daniel came in that evening, he paused in the doorway, taking in the spotless kitchen, the table set for company, and Grace's anxious face.

"You don't need to work so hard," he said quietly.

"I don't mind. I want to contribute. I want to be useful." Grace's voice was controlled, but Mrs. Clarkson's earlier concern had shaken her composure.

Daniel studied her face for a long moment, and Grace thought she saw something soften in his expression. But then he nodded and took his seat for supper.

By Thursday morning, Grace was exhausted. Every muscle in her body ached. She had been up until midnight baking and cleaning, determined to have everything perfect when Daniel came to the kitchen for breakfast.

But when she stumbled into the kitchen at dawn, she found he had already left to do the morning chores.

Grace made breakfast anyway, keeping it warm as the morning stretched on. When Daniel finally came in, nearly two hours later than usual, the food was overcooked and her nerves were frayed.

"I kept it warm," she said, trying to mask her disappointment as she served him rubbery eggs and dried-out bacon.

"You don't need to wait for me," Daniel said, but not unkindly. "I had to help birth a calf. These things can't wait for meal times."

Grace nodded, though she felt the hot tears building behind her eyes. Everything she tried seemed wrong. She was too much or not enough, and never quite what he needed.

As Daniel ate the overcooked breakfast without complaint, Grace busied herself wiping down surfaces that were already clean.

The silence stretched between them, heavy with unspoken words and hurt feelings.

"Grace." Daniel's voice made her turn. He was watching her with an expression she couldn't read. "You don't have to—"

The sound of a neighbor's wagon pulling into the yard interrupted him. Without another word, Daniel rose from the table and left the house. Grace felt both relief and disappointment as the moment between them passed.

By Friday, Grace gave up. They settled into a routine of polite distance. Daniel left before Grace woke and returned after she was asleep. Grace continued her frantic domestic activities, cooking elaborate meals that often went cold before Daniel returned to eat them.

She talked to the chickens as she collected eggs, carrying on the conversations she wished she could have had with her husband.

"I don't know what to do, ladies," she confided to the hens. "He won't talk to me, and I can't explain without making things worse. Mrs. Whiteman has poisoned everything with her gossip."

The chickens clucked in sympathy and continued their important work of scratching for bugs.

That evening, Grace waited until she heard Daniel's footsteps on the porch before lighting the lamp in the kitchen.

She served him supper of a beef roast with vegetables and fresh bread, and sat across from him with her own plate.

For a few minutes, they ate in silence. Then Daniel cleared his throat.

"The Clarkson's asked if we'd like to come for Sunday dinner," he said, not looking up from his plate.

Grace's heart jumped. It was the longest sentence he had spoken to her all week. "That sounds nice. Should I take something?"

"Mrs. Clarkson said not to worry about it." Daniel paused, seeming to struggle with something. "Grace, I—"

But his words didn't come. He shook his head and returned to his meal, leaving Grace wondering what he had been about to say.

As she washed the supper dishes, Grace caught sight of her reflection in the dark kitchen window. She looked pale and drawn, her eyes ringed with exhaustion and worry.

This couldn't continue. Something had to give, but Grace did not know how to bridge the growing chasm between them.

Outside, she could see Daniel's silhouette as he checked on the animals one last time before bed.

He moved with the calm confidence of a man comfortable in his own space, but even from a distance, Grace could see the tension in his shoulders.

They were both miserable, both hurting, but neither seemed to know how to reach across the divide that Mrs. Whiteman's gossip had created between them.

CHAPTER 14

On a seasonally cool Tuesday morning, Mrs. Clarkson arrived at dawn with her largest copper kettle and a determined smile.

"Apple butter day!" she announced cheerfully. "The trees are heavy with fruit, and we can't let it go to waste."

Grace welcomed the distraction from the tense silence that had settled over the farmhouse. She and Mrs. Clarkson worked together in tandem, peeling and coring baskets of apples while the large kettle bubbled over an outdoor fire.

"The secret is patience," Mrs. Clarkson explained as they stirred the thick, fragrant mixture. "Low heat and constant stirring for hours. No shortcuts if you want it smooth and rich."

Grace found the repetitive work soothing. The sweet smell of cinnamon and apples filled the air, and for a few hours, she could almost forget the growing distance between her and Daniel.

"You're getting quite skilled at this," Mrs. Clarkson observed as Grace expertly ladled the finished apple butter into waiting jars. "Your preserves will see you nicely through the winter."

They also prepared several jars of applesauce and spiced

apple rings, the kitchen windows fogging with steam from the canning process. Grace felt deep satisfaction watching the neat rows of sealed jars cooling on the counter, tangible proof of her growing domestic abilities.

"Mrs. Clarkson," Grace said as they cleaned up, "thank you for teaching me all of this. I never realized how much I didn't know about keeping a home."

The older woman patted her arm gently. "You're a quick learner, dear, and your intelligence serves you well. You bring your own strengths to the tasks at hand, and that's worth far more than you realize."

A FEW DAYS LATER, Mrs. Clarkson returned with her wagon. "We need more canning jars," she announced. "Pumpkin and squash season will be here before we know it, and Mrs. Kildare's sewing circle is meeting this afternoon. I thought you might like to join us."

Grace climbed up beside the older woman, grateful to escape the oppressive silence at home.

The ride to town was pleasant, with Mrs. Clarkson chattering about the upcoming harvest festival and what she was doing to prepare her chicken coop for winter.

At the Prescott General Store, the women purchased four cases of canning jars and more supplies. Grace noticed Mrs. Whiteman examining fabric at the far end of the store, but the woman ignored them.

"That's a blessing," Mrs. Clarkson murmured, following Grace's gaze. "Perhaps she's found someone else to occupy her attention."

~

THE SEWING CIRCLE met in Mrs. Kildare's parlor, a cozy room filled with comfortable chairs and good light from large windows.

Five women were already present when Grace and Mrs. Clarkson arrived, their hands busy with various needlework projects.

"Grace! How lovely to see you again," Mrs. Kildare said warmly. "Please sit here by the window. What are you working on today?"

Grace pulled out an embroidered pillowcase she had been stitching in the evenings. It was a delicate pattern of roses and vines worked in silk thread.

The women leaned forward to examine her work, their expressions full of admiration.

"My word, that's exquisite," exclaimed Mrs. Foster, the banker's wife. "Where did you learn such fine needlework?"

"My mother taught me," Grace replied. "She was very skilled with her needle."

"I should say so! This is the quality of work you'd see in the finest homes back East," added Mrs. Simmons, a farmer's wife. "You must teach my daughter! She can barely manage a straight seam."

For the first time in weeks, Grace felt herself relaxing. The women's praise was genuine, and she enjoyed their company as they worked and chatted about local news and family matters.

But then Agnes Whiteman arrived.

"Hello, ladies," she said, settling herself in the remaining chair with an exaggerated air of importance. "What a lovely gathering. Mrs. Carrington, how nice to see you again."

The atmosphere in the room shifted perceptibly. Grace could feel the other women's discomfort as Mrs. Whiteman's sharp eyes took in Grace's fine needlework.

"Such elegant stitching," Mrs. Whiteman observed. "Quite

above what one would expect from a local farmer's wife. Tell me, dear, where did you live before coming to Prescott?"

Grace's hands stilled on her embroidery. "Massachusetts," she mumbled.

"Yes, but where in Massachusetts? What was your father's profession again?"

Mrs. Clarkson cleared her throat. "Agnes, perhaps we should focus on our sewing. Mrs. Carrington is trying to concentrate on her work."

But Mrs. Whiteman pressed on. "I'm simply curious about our new neighbor's background. It's natural to want to know about the people living in our community." Her smile was sharp. "After all, some of us have been here for decades. We like to know who we're welcoming into our midst."

Grace felt heat creep up her neck. The other women looked uncomfortable, but none spoke up to deflect the questioning.

"I prefer not to dwell on the past," Grace said finally. "I'm here now, and that's what matters."

Mrs. Whiteman's eyebrows rose. "How mysterious. Most people are happy to share their family history. Unless of course there's something they'd rather not discuss."

The implication hung in the air and didn't go away. Grace could see doubt creeping into some of the women's expressions.

Her silence, meant to protect her privacy, was being interpreted as guilt.

THE REMAINDER of the sewing circle passed in awkward tension.

They praised Grace's needlework, but conversations ended when she tried to join them. By the time Mrs. Clarkson suggested they head home, Grace was thoroughly miserable.

"Don't let Agnes Whiteman ruin what should have been a pleasant afternoon," Mrs. Clarkson patted Grace's knee as they drove toward the farm. "The other women liked you very much."

"But they believed her insinuations," Grace said bitterly. "I could see it on their faces. My refusal to discuss my past only made me look more suspicious."

"Perhaps if you shared just a little..."

"What should I share?" Grace's voice rose in frustration. "That my uncle stole everything and sold me off to the highest bidder? That my husband was paid to take me because no one else would want me? That I'm nothing but a burden he's stuck with?"

Mrs. Clarkson was quiet for a moment. "Grace, we've talked about this before. I don't think—"

"I know what you think," Grace interrupted. "But you weren't there. You didn't hear my uncle explain exactly how worthless I am."

They completed the ride in silence, Grace's mood growing darker with each mile. By the time they reached the farm, she seethed with anger and hurt.

Daniel was just coming in from the barn when Grace climbed down from the wagon, her face set in hard lines.

He looked tired and dusty, and when he saw her expression, his own face closed off.

"How was town?" he asked.

"Wonderful," Grace replied sarcastically, brushing past him toward the house. "Your neighbors are so welcoming."

Daniel followed her into the kitchen, where Grace began yanking off her gloves with jerky movements.

"What happened?" he asked.

"Nothing I didn't expect," Grace said, not looking at him. "Just small-town gossips spreading their poison."

"Grace—"

"Don't." She held up a hand to stop him. "I'm not in the mood for conversation."

Daniel's jaw tightened. "Maybe if you talked to people instead of acting like you have something to hide—"

"Something to hide?" Grace whirled to face him. "Is that what you think, too?"

"I don't know what to think!" Daniel's voice rose. "You won't tell me anything! You act guilty about something, but you won't say what. How am I supposed to defend you when I don't know what I'm defending you from?"

Grace felt tears of rage and frustration burning her eyes. "Maybe you shouldn't bother defending me at all. Maybe you should just let them think whatever they want."

"And what about what I want to think?" Daniel stepped closer, his own anger building. "What about the fact that I'm your husband and I deserve to know the truth?"

"The truth?" Grace's laugh was bitter. "You want the truth? The truth is that you're stuck with me, whether you like it or not. The truth is that I'll never be the wife you wanted, and everyone in town knows it."

"That's not—"

"I'm tired, Daniel. I'm tired of pretending this is something it's not. I'm tired of trying to be grateful for scraps of kindness." Grace turned away from him, her voice breaking. "And I'm tired of cooking meals for someone who can't stand to be in the same room with me."

"What's that supposed to mean?"

"It means cook your own supper!" Grace snapped, reaching for one of the applesauce jars on the counter. "I'm done pretending to be the perfect farm wife for someone who wishes he'd never married me!"

She grabbed the jar roughly, and it slipped from her trembling fingers. The glass shattered against the kitchen floor, sending applesauce and sharp fragments everywhere.

"Now look what you've made me do!" Grace cried, dropping to her knees to gather the pieces.

"Grace, don't—"

But she was already reaching for the largest shard of glass, her vision blurred with tears. The sharp edge sliced deep into her palm, and she cried out as blood began to gush.

"Grace!" Daniel was beside her in an instant, pulling her away from the broken glass. "Let me see your hand!"

Blood was dripping through her fingers as Grace stared in shock. The cut was deep, running across her palm from her thumb to her little finger.

"I'm sorry," she whispered, suddenly deflated. "I'm sorry about the applesauce. I worked so hard on it, and now it's ruined, and I've made such a mess..."

"Forget the applesauce." Daniel hurriedly wrapped a kitchen towel around her bleeding hand. "We need to get you to the doctor."

As the reality of her injury sank in, Grace started to shake. The physical pain was nothing compared to the emotional wounds that had been festering for weeks, but somehow the sight of her own blood broke through her composure.

"I can't do this anymore," she whispered. "I can't pretend that everything is fine when it's not. I can't keep trying to earn something that was never freely given."

Daniel looked at her with confusion and concern, but there was no time for explanations. The cut was serious, and Grace was growing pale from blood loss.

The fight would have to wait. Right now, his wife needed medical attention.

CHAPTER 15

Dr. Kildare arrived within the hour, his black medical bag in hand and his weathered face creased with concern.

Daniel had wrapped Grace's hand as best he could, but blood had soaked through multiple towels during his ride to town to fetch the doctor.

"Let's have a look," Dr. Kildare said gently, unwrapping the makeshift bandage as Grace sat pale and shaking at the kitchen table.

"That's a deep one, Mrs. Carrington. You're going to need quite a few stitches."

Grace winced as he cleaned the wound, the pain sharp enough to cut through her emotional numbness.

Daniel stood behind her chair, his hands hovering near her shoulders but not quite touching.

"Hold still now," the doctor murmured, threading his needle. "This will hurt, but it's necessary."

Grace gripped the edge of the table with her good hand, silent tears streaming down her face, although whether from physical pain or emotional exhaustion, she couldn't say.

As each stitch was pulled tight, she leaned back against Daniel's solid presence despite everything that had passed between them.

"There," Dr. Kildare said, wrapping her palm in clean white bandages. "Eleven stitches. Keep it dry and clean. I'll come back and check on you in a few days."

He packed up his instruments, then paused. "Mrs. Carrington, you've lost quite a bit of blood. You need bed rest and proper food. No heavy work for at least a week."

The doctor turned to Daniel. "Your wife needs to go to bed right away, and she needs to stay there. She needs rest in order for her body to replenish the blood that's been lost. Do you understand?"

Daniel nodded silently, his face pinched with worry.

After the doctor left, silence settled over the kitchen. Grace stared at her bandaged hand and tried to flex her fingers, wincing at the pull of the stitches.

"Grace," Daniel said quietly, "we need to talk for a minute, and then I'll help you to bed."

Daniel pulled a chair close to hers and sat down, his elbows on his knees, his expression more serious than she had ever seen it.

"What you said earlier, about trying to earn something that was never freely given. What did you mean?"

Grace looked down at her bandaged hand, her throat tight with unshed tears. "It doesn't matter."

"It matters to me." Daniel's voice was gentle but firm. "Grace, I've watched you work yourself to death trying to be perfect. I've seen you jump every time I walk into a room, like you're waiting for me to tell you to leave. I don't understand why you think you have to earn your place here."

Grace was quiet for so long that Daniel wondered if she

would answer at all. When she spoke, her voice was barely above a whisper.

"He told me that you were paid to take me."

Daniel went still. "What?"

"My uncle." Grace's words came out in a rush now, as if a dam had broken. "He said no man would want me for myself. He said I was a burden with no skills and expensive tastes, and that he had to pay you three hundred dollars to marry me. He said you were doing him a favor by taking me off his hands."

The color drained from Daniel's face. "Grace, that's not—I received no money. Not one penny."

Grace looked up at him then, confusion and hope warring in her eyes. "But he said—"

"Your uncle lied to you." Daniel's voice was hard with anger, but not at her. "Grace, I chose to find a wife. I advertised for a mail-order bride because I wanted a partner, someone to share my life with. No one paid me anything."

"But why would he lie about that?"

Daniel was quiet for a moment, his jaw working as he thought. "Maybe because he knew it made you feel worthless. Maybe because it gave him control over you."

He leaned forward. "Grace, exactly what happened after your father died?"

Grace told him everything.

She told him about Uncle's immediate arrival after her father's sudden death, and how he had taken over the house and seized all the accounts.

She wept when she told him about finding her mother's jewelry box empty and the confrontation over the pearl necklace.

She told him about the necklace breaking and the precious pearls scattering across the floor, and how Uncle had swept up the remaining pieces in order to stop her from trying to save them.

She told him about the five pearls she had hidden in her dress lining, the only remnants of her mother's memory that Uncle hadn't been able to steal.

She spoke of the forced marriage arrangement, of believing she was being sold like livestock, of the shame that had eaten at her every day since arriving in Prescott.

Daniel listened without interruption, his expression growing darker with each revelation.

When Grace finished, her voice hoarse from talking, he was silent for a long moment.

"Grace, I'm so sorry. I did not know what you went through."

"Mrs. Clarkson tried to tell me," Grace admitted. "She said you weren't the kind of man who would marry for money. But I couldn't believe it. Uncle was so convincing, and I felt so worthless."

"You're not worthless." The look on Daniel's face was furious. "You're smart and brave and kind. You faced down a snake in my chicken coop without blinking. You learned to cook and manage a household in a matter of weeks. You've made this house feel like a home for the first time in years."

Grace felt fresh tears starting. "But I've been so difficult and so defensive. I kept waiting for you to show your true feelings about being stuck with me."

"The only thing I've been stuck with is not knowing how to help you." Daniel reached out and slowly took her uninjured hand. "Grace, when I decided to find a wife, I hoped for someone exactly like you. Someone with education and refinement, yes, but also someone who would appreciate what I could offer instead of always wanting more."

"Priscilla," Grace said, remembering what Mrs. Clarkson had told her.

Daniel nodded. "She left because farm life wasn't exciting enough. She wanted city living, travel, fine things I couldn't give her. When I wrote to you, or thought I was writing to you, I hoped I was finding someone who would value a simple life, someone looking for a real home."

"Uncle wrote those letters," Grace said. "I never saw them."

"Then he knew what I was looking for." Daniel's thumb traced over her knuckles. "Grace, everything I've learned about you since you arrived has made me glad I married you. Even when you were burning breakfast and soaking me with milk."

Despite everything, Grace smiled at the memory. "I was terrible at everything."

"You were learning. And you never gave up." Daniel's expression grew serious again. "Grace, I want you to listen to me carefully. You are not a burden. You are wanted. You are my wife because I chose you, and I'm grateful every day that you're here with me."

Grace stared at their joined hands, hardly daring to believe what she was hearing. "Even after today? After the things I said?"

"Especially after today." Daniel squeezed her fingers gently. "You were hurt and angry, and you had every right to be. Your uncle lied to you about one of the most important things in your life, and I've been too blind to see how much pain you were carrying."

"I wanted to tell you," Grace whispered. "So many times I almost did. But I was afraid—"

"Of what?"

"That if you knew how little Uncle valued me, you might start to see me the same way."

Daniel was quiet for a moment, and when he spoke, his voice was thick with emotion.

"Grace, your uncle was wrong about everything. You're not worthless. You're not a burden. And you certainly didn't need to be paid for." He paused. "In fact, I think I got the better end of this bargain by far."

Grace looked up at him then, really looked at him, and saw nothing but kindness in his eyes.

For the first time since arriving in Prescott, she believed that maybe, just maybe, she was wanted after all.

"What happens now?" she asked.

"Now we start over," Daniel said simply. "No more secrets, no more walking on eggshells. We learn to be a proper married couple, without your uncle's lies standing between us."

Grace nodded, feeling lighter than she had in weeks despite the throbbing in her bandaged hand. "I'd like that."

"Good." Daniel smiled then, the first real smile she'd seen from him in over two weeks. "Because I've been waiting to get to know my wife. The real Grace, not the one trying so hard to be perfect all the time."

As the last of the evening light slanted through the kitchen windows, illuminating the broken glass still scattered on the floor, Grace felt something broken inside her begin to mend as well.

There would be more to work through, more conversations to have, but for the first time since her father's death, she felt like she might have found a home.

"Daniel?" her voice was soft.

"Yes?"

"Thank you for taking care of me today." She gestured helplessly with her good hand. "For getting the doctor, for listening, for..."

"For what?"

"For wanting me anyway."

Daniel stood and leaned down to press a gentle kiss to the top of her head.

"Grace Carrington," he said quietly, "I can't imagine wanting anyone more."

CHAPTER 16

The rooster crowing woke the farm the next morning, and Grace lay in bed for a few minutes, listening to the sound of Daniel moving around the kitchen.

Her bandaged hand throbbed, and her entire arm was stiff to the point of being unmovable, but for the first time in weeks her heart felt light.

The weight of Uncle's lies were gone, replaced by something she had never dared hope for—the knowledge that she was wanted.

She made her way downstairs and found Daniel at the stove, tending to ham and eggs. He looked up as she entered, his face breaking into a shy smile.

"Good morning, but you're supposed to be in bed." He turned away from the stove to pull out a chair for her. "How does your hand feel?"

"It's pretty sore." Grace settled into the chair, holding her hand to her breast for stability. She watched him move back to the pan of eggs.

There was an ease to his movements now, a relaxation in his

shoulders that hadn't been there yesterday. "You didn't have to cook."

"I want to." Daniel glanced at her with a grin. "Besides, someone once told me that marriage is about learning together. I figure it's time I learned a few things, too."

Grace felt tears prick her eyes, but they were good tears this time. "Daniel, about yesterday—"

"No apologies," he said, bringing her a plate of cooked eggs and a slice of crisp ham. "We both said things that needed saying. Now we know where we stand."

As they ate breakfast together, Grace marveled at how different everything felt. The kitchen looked the same, but the oppressive tension was gone.

Daniel told her about another calf that had been born during the night, and shared his plans for expanding the chicken coop before winter set in.

"I was thinking," Daniel said, buttering a biscuit, "maybe you'd like to help me choose the new chickens. You seem to have a way with them."

Grace smiled, remembering her encounter with Pearl in the first week. "I'd like that very much."

Over the next few days, Grace discovered what it meant to be Daniel's partner rather than his reluctant burden.

Due to her injured hand, Grace couldn't do much of anything at all, so Daniel insisted she rest while he took care of the morning chores. But instead of leaving her behind in the afternoon, he began asking for her company.

"Want to come with me to check the south pasture?" he asked one day after lunch, offering her his arm. "The walk will do you good, and I could use another pair of eyes to look at that fence."

Grace walked beside her husband through the crisp air,

their conversation flowing easily for the first time since their wedding.

Daniel pointed out how much bigger the new chicken coop would be as he shared stories about the land. He asked for her opinion on everything from putting in a few more apple trees to the best placement for a new well.

"You really want to know what I think?" Grace asked, surprised when he considered her suggestion about relocating a gate.

"Of course I do." Daniel looked at her with genuine confusion. "Grace, you've got a quick mind, and you're observant. Why wouldn't I want your input?"

It was such a simple statement, but it filled Grace with warmth. Uncle had convinced her that her thoughts and opinions were useless, but Daniel treated them as valuable.

With Grace unable to do heavy kitchen work, Daniel surprised her by suggesting they cook together.

"I'm hungry for your beef stew," he said one afternoon. "I can handle the chopping and stirring if you want to direct the cooking lesson."

Grace perched on a kitchen chair, bandaged hand elevated on a pillow in her lap, and called out directions.

Daniel chopped the vegetables and browned the beef. He followed her instructions without question, even when she suggested adding more seasoning.

"A little more salt," Grace said, tasting the broth from the spoon Daniel held out to her. "And maybe another bay leaf."

"Yes, ma'am," Daniel replied with mock seriousness, making her laugh.

The stew turned out better than the last batch Grace made, and as they sat down to eat, Daniel raised his coffee cup in a toast.

"To the most patient teacher I've ever had."

Grace blushed with pleasure. "I hardly did anything. You did all the work."

"I followed orders. You knew what needed to be done." Daniel's expression grew serious. "Grace, do you know how good it feels to work with you instead of thinking I must tread carefully around you?"

The honesty in his voice made Grace's throat tighten. "I'm sorry I made you feel you had to walk on eggshells."

"We both made mistakes," Daniel said gently. "But we're fixing them now."

The biggest change was in their evenings. Instead of Daniel retreating to the barn or Grace disappearing upstairs early, they began spending time together in the parlor.

Grace worked on her embroidery or knit, while Daniel read the weekly newspaper aloud, sharing local news and asking for her thoughts on various topics.

One evening, as Grace hemmed a new pillowcase with her good hand, Daniel set down his paper and watched her work.

"That's beautiful," he said, admiring the delicate rose pattern taking shape under her fingers. "Where did you learn to sew like that?"

"My mother taught me," Grace replied, her voice tight with memory. "She said needlework was a way to create beauty even in difficult times."

Daniel was quiet for a moment. "She sounds like a wise woman."

"She was." Grace looked up from her work. "I wish you could have met her. She would have liked you."

"What makes you say that?"

Grace pondered the question. "She always said the measure of a man was how he treated those who couldn't do anything for him. You've been nothing but kind to me, even when you thought I was hiding something from you."

Daniel leaned forward in his chair. "Grace, I want you to understand something. Even when I was frustrated with you, even when I didn't understand what was wrong, I never stopped wanting you here. I was just...lost. I didn't know how to help you."

Grace smiled shyly. "We were both lost. I'm glad we found each other."

CHAPTER 17

Not long after Grace's accident, Reverend Shoemaker's buggy rolled up the lane to the Carrington farm.

Grace, her hand still bandaged and aching, watched from the kitchen window with a mixture of surprise and apprehension.

"Someone's here," she called to Daniel, who was splitting wood near the barn.

Her husband straightened, shading his eyes against the afternoon sun. "That's the Reverend. Wonder what brings him out this way."

Grace's heart began to pound. Had Mrs. Whiteman already spread more gossip? Had the story of her accident reached town, twisted into yet another scandal?

Reverend Shoemaker climbed down from his buggy with the careful movements of a man who spent more time with books than with horses. His round, kind face broke into a warm smile as Daniel approached.

"Daniel! Good to see you, my boy. I hope I'm not intruding."

"Not at all, Reverend. What brings you out?"

"I heard Mrs. Carrington had an accident. Dr. Kildare mentioned it when I saw him at the general store. I thought I'd stop by to see how she's faring and offer any comfort I might be able to provide."

Daniel's expression softened. "That's kind of you, Sir. Come in, please. Grace will be glad to see you."

But Grace wasn't sure she was glad at all. As she heard the men's footsteps on the porch, she fought the urge to flee upstairs.

Her emotions were still too raw, too close to the surface. She didn't think she could maintain the polite facade that proper society required.

The door opened and Reverend Shoemaker entered, removing his hat. His eyes were full of genuine warmth and concern as they found her standing by the table.

"Mrs. Carrington! How are you feeling, my dear?"

"I'm well, Reverend. Thank you for coming." Grace's voice sounded hollow even to her own ears.

"I'll put on some coffee," Daniel said, moving toward the stove, but Reverend Shoemaker held up a hand.

"Actually, Daniel, if you don't mind, I'd like to speak with your wife privately for a few moments. Pastoral matters, you understand."

Daniel glanced at Grace, who gave a small nod, and he stepped outside, closing the door softly behind him.

Reverend Shoemaker settled himself at the kitchen table, gesturing for Grace to sit across from him. "Now then, Dr. Kildare said you cut your hand quite badly. May I see?"

Grace reluctantly held out her bandaged palm. "It was foolish. I dropped a jar and tried to pick up the broken glass."

"Mmm." The Reverend studied her face rather than her hand. "And how did this foolish accident happen?"

"I--I was cleaning up and I wasn't paying attention--"

"Mrs. Carrington." His voice was gentle but firm. "I've been a minister for thirty years. I've sat at more kitchen tables than I can count, and I've learned to recognize when an accident is just an accident, and when it's the physical manifestation of a much deeper wound."

Grace felt her carefully constructed composure begin to crack. "I don't know what you mean."

"I think you do." Reverend Shoemaker folded his hands on the table. "Grace...may I call you Grace? I've noticed you at services in the past weeks. I've seen how you sit so still, like you're trying to make yourself invisible. I've watched you flinch when certain people look your way. And I've observed the whispers that follow you."

Tears began to well in Grace's eyes despite her best efforts to hold them back.

"I've also noticed," the Reverend continued tenderly, "that you carry yourself like someone who expects to be struck. Not physically, perhaps, but struck nonetheless. And when Dr. Kildare mentioned your accident, he said you'd lost quite a bit of blood before your husband could get you help. He said you seemed almost...relieved by the pain."

"That's not..." Grace's voice broke. "I didn't mean to..."

"I'm not accusing you of anything, my child. I'm simply saying that in my experience, people don't cut themselves that badly by accident unless they're already deeply wounded inside."

And suddenly, as if a dam had burst, Grace found herself telling him everything.

The words poured out in a rush--about Uncle's cruelty, about the stolen jewelry and the broken pearl necklace, about the forced marriage and the lie about the dowry.

She told him about Mrs. Whiteman's vicious gossip, about

the sideways glances and whispered speculation, about how she'd worked herself to exhaustion trying to prove her worth.

"When Daniel asked me why I was acting like I had to earn my place here," Grace said, tears streaming down her face now. "We argued, and I said things, terrible things, and I was so angry and hurt that I grabbed the jar without thinking. It slipped and broke, and when I tried to clean it up, I was crying so hard I could barely see. The glass cut me, and there was so much blood, and I just--I couldn't anymore. I couldn't keep pretending."

She looked down at her bandaged hand, her voice dropping to a whisper. "Dr. Kildare said the cut was dangerous. He said if it had been just a little deeper, or if Daniel hadn't gotten him here so quickly, I could have..."

Grace couldn't finish the sentence.

Reverend Shoemaker was quiet for a long moment. When he spoke, his voice was thick with emotion.

"Grace, do you understand how serious this is? Not just the physical danger, but what drove you to that point?"

"I know. I know it was foolish and reckless and--"

"That's not what I meant." He leaned forward, his weathered face full of compassion. "I mean that the cruelty and lies that were inflicted on you, first by your uncle, then by the gossips in this town—that malice nearly cost you your life. That burden should have never been yours to carry alone."

Grace stared at him, fresh tears spilling over.

"Your uncle lied to you," Reverend Shoemaker said firmly. "He told you that you were worthless, that no one would want you, that your husband had to be paid to take you. Then members of my congregation, people who should have shown you Christian charity and welcome, chose instead to whisper and speculate and judge. They took your silence for guilt, your privacy for scandal, and your refinement for pretense."

He shook his head sadly. “The weight of all the lies and cruel assumptions bore down on you until you couldn't carry it anymore. It manifested in a moment of such pain and anger that you nearly bled to death on your own kitchen floor."

Grace covered her face with her good hand, sobbing openly now.

"But here's what I want you to know, Grace Carrington," the Reverend said, his voice growing stronger. "None of it was true. Not your uncle's assessment of your worth, not the town's assumptions about your character, and not your own belief that you had to earn the right to be loved."

He waited until Grace looked up at him, her face streaked with tears.

"You are a child of God and wonderfully made. You have an inherent worth that no uncle can steal and no gossip can diminish. And from what I've observed of your husband, he knows this far better than you've given him credit for."

"He said he never received any money," Grace whispered. "He said my uncle lied about everything."

"And do you believe him now?"

Grace nodded slowly. "We talked after the doctor left. Really talked, for the first time since I arrived. He was so kind, so patient. He said he chose me, that he wanted me here." Fresh tears welled up. "I've been such a fool, Reverend. I believed Uncle's lies over Daniel's actions."

"You believed what you had been taught to believe," Reverend Shoemaker corrected gently. "When someone we should be able to trust, like an uncle, tells us we're worthless often enough, we start to see worthlessness everywhere, even where it doesn't exist."

The minister pulled a clean handkerchief from his pocket and handed it to Grace. "But now you know the truth. Your uncle was a cruel, greedy man who used lies to control you, and the gossips in town are small-minded people who fill their empty lives with speculation about others. Neither group deserves the power you've given them."

Grace dabbed at her eyes with the handkerchief. "But what do I do now? Mrs. Whiteman won't stop talking. Even if Daniel and I are better, the whole town still thinks--"

"Let me worry about Mrs. Whiteman," Reverend Shoemaker said, and there was a note of steel beneath his gentle tone that Grace had never heard before. "I've been too patient with that woman's sharp tongue for too long. It's time someone reminded the congregation what the Good Book says about gossip and bearing false witness."

Grace looked up in surprise.

"You see, Grace, you're not the only one who's been wounded by wagging tongues in this town. But you are the only one who nearly paid the ultimate price for it. And that..." His jaw set firmly. "That I cannot and will not tolerate."

The man stood, placing a fatherly hand on Grace's shoulder. "You rest and heal, both in body and in spirit. Talk with your husband. Learn to trust the love he's offering you. And come Sunday, you come to church with your head held high, because you have absolutely nothing to be ashamed of."

"But Mrs. Whiteman--"

"Will hear a sermon she won't soon forget," Reverend Shoemaker said grimly. "I've been praying for guidance on how to address the spirit of gossip and judgment that's taken root in my congregation. Your story has shown me just how urgent that need has become."

He collected his hat and moved toward the door, then paused.

"Grace, may I ask you something?"

"Of course, Reverend."

"Do you still have those five pearls? The ones you saved from your mother's necklace?"

Grace's hand instinctively went to her bodice, where the small linen packet rested against her heart. "Yes. They're all I have left of her."

"Good." Reverend Shoemaker smiled. "Hold onto them. Not because they're valuable, though they are, but because they're a reminder. Your mother's love wasn't diminished by being scattered. Those five pearls are just as precious as fifty would be. Your worth is not diminished by the lies others have told about you."

After he left, Grace sat at the kitchen table for a long time, staring at her bandaged hand. Daniel came in quietly and sat beside her, not speaking, just being present.

"He knows," Grace said finally. "I told him everything."

"Good," Daniel replied simply, taking her uninjured hand in his. "It's time the truth came out. All of it."

CHAPTER 18

Sunday dawned clear and cold, the kind of November morning that promised winter's approach.

Grace dressed with trembling hands, choosing her most modest dress--a deep brown wool with a simple black collar.

"You don't have to do this," Daniel said, watching her struggle with the buttons. "We can stay home if you're not ready."

"No." Grace's voice was firm despite her nervousness. "Reverend Shoemaker said to come with my head held high. I'm tired of hiding."

As their wagon pulled up to the church, Grace noticed the difference immediately. Mrs. Clarkson hurried over with a warm smile, offering Grace her arm. Mrs. Kildare, the doctor's wife, waved from the church steps. Mr. Zimmerman from the general store tipped his hat respectfully.

But Grace also saw Mrs. Whiteman standing near the entrance, her thin face set in its usual expression of sour disapproval, her eyes sharp and calculating as always.

Daniel helped Grace down from the wagon, his hand firm

and supportive at her elbow. Together they walked toward the church, and Grace noticed that people seemed to be watching them with unusual interest, not the cruel speculation she'd grown accustomed to, but something else. Curiosity, perhaps. Or anticipation.

Inside, Mrs. Clarkson guided them to a pew near the front. "We saved you seats with us," she whispered, and Grace saw that several of the kinder townspeople had clustered nearby, as if forming a protective circle.

Behind them, Grace heard the rustle of Mrs. Whiteman settling into her usual pew, the third row, where she'd sat for twenty years, surrounded by her small cadre of fellow gossips.

The organ began to play, and Reverend Shoemaker took his place at the pulpit. But instead of his usual warm smile, his expression was grave, almost sorrowful.

"My dear friends," he began, his voice carrying clearly through the small church, "today I must speak to you about a matter that weighs heavily on my heart. Please turn with me to James, Chapter Three."

He opened his Bible with deliberate care. "Starting at Verse Five: 'Likewise, the tongue is a small part of the body, but it makes great boasts. Consider what a great forest is set on fire by a small spark. The tongue also is a fire, a world of evil among the parts of the body. It corrupts the whole body, sets the whole course of one's life on fire, and is itself set on fire by hell.'"

Grace felt Daniel's hand find hers, squeezing gently. Around them, the congregation had gone very still.

"Strong words," Reverend Shoemaker continued, closing the Bible but keeping his hand on it. "Words that speak to a truth we often forget: that our tongues, these small, seemingly insignificant parts of our bodies, have the power to create or to destroy. To heal or to wound. To build up or to tear down."

He paused, his eyes sweeping the congregation, lingering for a moment on Mrs. Whiteman's rigid figure.

"This week, I sat in a kitchen not far from here and listened to a young woman tell me her story. A story of cruelty and lies, of manipulation and theft. A story of how she was told, by someone who should have protected her, that she was worthless. She was told she was useless, and that no one would want her except as a burden to be paid for."

Grace felt her cheeks flush, but Reverend Shoemaker's voice was gentle, not exposing but explaining.

"And then this young woman came to our town, carrying those lies on her heart like stones. Believing herself unwanted. Believing herself a burden. She worked herself to exhaustion to prove a worth that was never in question."

Mrs. Clarkson squeezed Grace's other hand in support.

"But the lies from her past were not the worst of her burdens," Reverend Shoemaker said, and now his voice grew harder. "No, that weight was added by members of this very congregation. People who saw a young woman with education and refinement and decided, with no evidence, no knowledge, and no Christian charity, that there must be something scandalous in her past."

The silence in the church was profound. Grace could hear her own heartbeat.

"They whispered in shops and at sewing circles. They speculated about her character, her motives, and her morals. They saw her privacy as proof of guilt. They interpreted her silence as confirmation of their worst imaginings. And they spread their poison with such conviction that even her own husband began to doubt."

Grace heard a sharp intake of breath from somewhere behind them. Mrs. Whiteman, perhaps, realizing where this sermon was heading.

"And do you know what happened?" Reverend Shoemaker's voice broke slightly. "This young woman, already wounded by her uncle's cruelty, bearing the weight of genuine loss and trauma, crushed beneath the burden of small-town gossip...well, she cut her hand so badly while in an emotional crisis that she nearly bled to death."

Gasps rippled through the congregation. Grace felt tears sliding down her cheeks as Daniel's arm came around her shoulders.

"Dr. Kildare told me," Reverend Shoemaker continued, "that if the cut had been slightly deeper, or if her husband had been slower to get help, we would have been planning a funeral this week instead of having this conversation. A young woman's life nearly ended because the weight of lies--both from her past and from our present--became too heavy to bear."

He let that sink in, his gaze moving from face to face.

"Now, I want to be very clear about something. This young woman, Grace Carrington, is guilty of nothing except trusting the wrong people and believing the lies they told her about herself. Her past contains no scandal, no disgrace, no shame. She is a banker's daughter who lost her father suddenly. She was robbed by a cruel uncle, and then forced into a marriage she believed was a business transaction."

Reverend Shoemaker's voice softened. "But that marriage? It was no transaction. Her husband never received a penny. He hoped for a partner to share his life with. He chose her, and he's been bewildered by her defensive behavior ever since her arrival. Because while he was trying to build a marriage, she was trying to earn the right to exist."

Grace buried her face in Daniel's shoulder, overwhelmed by the public validation of her pain.

"So I ask you, members of this congregation: When you whispered about Grace Carrington, did you build up the body of

Christ? When you speculated about her past, did you show Christian charity? When you saw her struggling and chose to judge rather than help, did you act as Christ would have acted?"

The silence was damning.

"The Bible tells us in Proverbs Chapter 18:21 that 'Death and life are in the power of the tongue.' Every time we speak, we choose which we will spread. And this week, I saw firsthand the death that our tongues nearly caused."

Reverend Shoemaker's expression grew fierce. "I will not have it. Not in my church. Not in my congregation. Not among people who claim to follow a Christ who ate with sinners and defended the accused woman from her stone-throwing judges."

He opened his Bible again. "Matthew 7, verses 1 through 3: 'Do not judge, or you too will be judged. For in the same way you judge others, you will be judged, and with the measure you use, it will be measured to you. Why do you look at the speck of sawdust in your brother's eye and pay no attention to the plank in your own eye?'"

His eyes found Mrs. Whiteman in the third row. "There are those among us who have made a practice of finding a splinter in others' eyes while carrying entire lumber yards in their own. There are those who have elevated gossip to an art form and wielded speculation like a weapon. Those who have measured others with harsh judgment while demanding grace for themselves."

Mrs. Whiteman's face had gone from pale to crimson.

"To those people, I say this: Your season of influence is over. Your words carry no weight in a congregation that values truth and charity. And if you continue to spread poison with your tongues, you will find yourself sitting alone, because the good people of this community have had enough."

He closed the Bible with finality. "And to the rest of you, those who participated passively in gossip, who listened to speculation without challenging it, who saw a young woman struggling and offered judgment instead of help, I say this: Repent. Go to Grace Carrington and ask her forgiveness. Show her the Christian charity you should have shown from the beginning. And in the future, when you're tempted to whisper about another person's circumstances, remember how close your loose tongues came to costing a life."

Reverend Shoemaker's voice gentled. "Grace, Daniel, would you stand please?"

Grace's heart pounded as Daniel helped her to her feet. She kept her eyes down, unable to meet the gaze of the congregation.

"Look at me, child," Reverend Shoemaker said kindly, and Grace slowly raised her eyes to his. "These are your neighbors. Your community. Your brothers and sisters in Christ. They owe you an apology."

For a long moment, no one moved. Then Mrs. Kildare stood, tears streaming down her face. "Grace, I am so sorry. I never repeated the gossip, but I didn't stop it either. Please forgive me."

Mrs. Clarkson rose next, her hand reaching for Grace's. "I tried to defend you, dear, but I should have done more. I should have spoken louder. I'm sorry."

One by one, people began to stand--some crying, some looking ashamed, all offering apologies. Even Mr. Zimmerman stood, hat in hand. "I heard things said in my store and I didn't put a stop to it. That ends today."

Only Mrs. Whiteman remained seated, her face a mask of rigid fury, surrounded now by empty space as her former allies all stood together to apologize.

After the service, something remarkable happened. Instead of the usual quick departure, people lingered. They approached Grace with genuine warmth, offering invitations to dinner, asking about her hand, welcoming her properly to the community.

Mrs. Kildare took both of Grace's hands in hers. "My sewing circle meets Thursday. Would you honor us with your presence? We could use your skill with a needle."

"I'd love to," Grace said, her voice thick with emotion.

As people gathered around Grace and Daniel, Mrs. Whiteman stood alone by her wagon. No one approached her. No one sought her opinion. No one even looked her way.

She climbed into her wagon with jerky, graceless movements, her husband already seated and clearly eager to leave. As they drove past, Mrs. Whiteman stared straight ahead, her chin lifted in defiant pride, but Grace could see the tremor in her rigid shoulders.

"Do you feel sorry for her?" Daniel asked quietly, watching the wagon disappear.

Grace considered this. "A little. But mostly I feel sorry that she's spent so long tearing others down that she doesn't know how to build anything up. Including herself."

Reverend Shoemaker appeared at her elbow. "How are you feeling, my dear?"

"Overwhelmed," Grace admitted. "But good. I feel good."

"Excellent." He smiled. "And Mrs. Whiteman?"

"I do feel sorry for her. Will she..." Grace hesitated. "Will they forgive her? Eventually?"

"If she shows genuine repentance and changes her ways, yes. That's what we do as Christians." Reverend Shoemaker's expression grew serious. "But I won't hold my breath. Women like Agnes Whiteman rarely believe they've done anything wrong. They see themselves as the gatekeepers of morality and of propriety. They never recognize their cruelty for what it is."

~

Over the following weeks, the transformation in Prescott was remarkable. Grace found herself genuinely welcomed into the community.

The sewing circle became a source of friendship and laughter. Invitations to dinner and social events multiplied. Everywhere Grace went, people treated her with the respect and warmth that had been missing before.

Mrs. Whiteman, meanwhile, faded into social obscurity. She still attended church, still came to town, but she sat alone, spoke to few, and was consulted by none. The mantle of social influence she'd worn for twenty years had been stripped away, and nothing remained but a bitter woman growing old in an isolation of her own making.

Grace, watching Mrs. Whiteman's lonely figure from across the churchyard one Sunday, felt something unexpected: not triumph, but a quiet sadness for a soul that had chosen judgment over grace, cruelty over kindness, and pride over repentance.

But she also felt something else, something stronger and brighter. She felt free. Free from the lies, free from the shame, free from the weight of trying to earn worth that had been rightfully hers all along.

She slipped her hand into Daniel's as they walked to their wagon, and when she felt the small linen packet of pearls resting against her heart, she smiled.

Five pearls, scattered yet saved. Just like her life, broken by cruelty but made whole by love.

And that, Grace thought as Daniel helped her into the wagon, was more than enough.

CHAPTER 19

Almost three weeks after Grace's accident, when she could use both hands again, she surprised Daniel by making his favorite apple pie.

She was rolling out the crust when her husband came in from the barn, covered in mud from helping a cow who had gotten stuck in a marshy spot near the creek.

"Don't come any closer!" Grace warned, brandishing her rolling pin. "I've got this crust perfect, and you're dripping all over my clean floor."

Daniel stopped in the doorway, grinning at her mock-fierce expression. "Yes, ma'am. But I just wanted to tell you that Pearl got herself stuck again. Took me an hour to get her out."

"That cow is more trouble than she's worth," Grace said, transferring the crust to her pie tin.

"Don't let her hear you say that. She's very sensitive about her dignity." Daniel's deadpan delivery made Grace snort with laughter.

"Her dignity? Daniel Carrington, that cow has no dignity. I've had to chase her away when she tried to eat my laundry off the line."

"Well, in her defense, your aprons do smell like pie."

Grace dissolved into genuine laughter, the kind that came from deep in her belly and brought tears to her eyes. Daniel watched her with such delight that she laughed even harder.

"What?" she gasped, wiping her eyes with her wrist.

"I've never heard you really laugh before. It's a wonderful sound."

Grace felt her cheeks warm, but not with embarrassment this time. With happiness.

As late October's first frost touched the windows, Grace and Daniel continued making plans together. Winter on the plains took planning in order to survive.

"I was thinking about what Mrs. Clarkson said," Grace mentioned one evening as they sat by the fire. "About helping Miss Crawford with the school children. Would you mind if I spoke to her about it?"

"I think it's a wonderful idea," Daniel replied. "You'd be good with children, and they'd benefit from your education."

"I could teach the younger ones their letters," Grace said, warming to the idea. "And maybe help with arithmetic. I always enjoyed working with numbers."

Daniel smiled. "Your father taught you well with those ledgers."

"He did." Grace's voice was wistful, but no longer pained. "He always said education was the one thing no one could take away from you."

"He was right about that." Daniel reached over and took her hand. "Grace, I want you to know that whatever you want to do, teaching, helping in the community, learning new skills, I'll support you. This is your home too, and you should have a say in how you spend your days."

Grace squeezed his fingers, marveling at how natural it felt to hold his hand now.

"Thank you. That means everything to me."

One evening in early November, as they sat by the fire, Grace found the courage to ask what had been growing in her heart.

"Daniel," she whispered, holding her needlework close, "do you think...do you think we might learn to love each other? At some point? Truly love each other, I mean?"

Daniel set down his book and turned to face her. "Grace, can I tell you something?"

She nodded, her heart beating fast.

"I think I'm already halfway there," he said quietly. "Maybe more than halfway. When I saw you bleeding the day you cut your hand, when I thought you might be seriously hurt? I've never been so scared in my life."

Grace felt tears spring to her eyes. "Really?"

"Really." Daniel moved to sit beside her on the sofa. "I know we started this marriage for practical reasons, but somewhere along the way, you became important to me. Not just as a wife or a helper, but as you. Grace. The woman who faces down snakes and chases the milk cow and makes this house a home."

"I think I love you too," Grace whispered. "I was just afraid to admit it, even to myself."

Daniel cupped her face gently with his hands. "We don't have to be afraid anymore. We know the truth now. It's time we build something real between us."

When he kissed her this time, it wasn't the brief, formal kiss of their wedding day. It was the kiss of a man who loved his wife, and a woman who had learned she was worthy of being chosen.

As December approached, Grace noticed Daniel making mysterious trips to town and having quiet conversations with Mrs. Clarkson that stopped when Grace was near. She might have worried about such secrecy before, but now she trusted her husband completely.

"Are you planning something for Christmas?" she asked one evening, catching him hiding what looked like a small package.

Daniel's guilty expression was so endearing that Grace laughed.

"Don't try to deny it. You're terrible at keeping secrets."

"Maybe I am," Daniel said with a grin. "But this one's worth keeping. You'll just have to wait and see."

Grace settled back in her chair with her sewing, gratitude flooding her being. For the first time since her father's death, she was looking forward to Christmas.

Not because she expected gifts or grand celebrations, but because she would spend it with a man who loved her, and whom she loved in return.

Whatever Daniel was planning, she knew it would be perfect, because it would come from his heart. And that was all she had ever wanted—to be loved not out of obligation or payment, but out of genuine affection and choice.

The terrified girl who had knelt on her uncle's floor, gathering scattered pearls like broken dreams, was gone.

In her place was a woman who knew her own worth, a wife who was wanted, and a partner who was building something beautiful with the man she loved.

CHAPTER 20

Christmas Eve arrived crisp and cold. Grace dressed to the sound of Daniel humming in the kitchen, something she had never heard him do before.

Snow had fallen during the night, blanketing the farm in pristine white that sparkled like scattered diamonds in the morning sun. The world looked new, clean, and full of promise.

Wearing her best green wool day dress, Grace made her way downstairs, following the scent of coffee and something sweet baking in the oven.

"Merry Christmas Eve," Daniel said, turning from the stove with a smile that made her heart flutter. "I thought I'd surprise you with those molasses cookies you said your mother used to make."

Grace's throat tightened with emotion. She had mentioned the cookies only once, weeks ago, during one of their evening conversations. That he had remembered and taken the time to make them for her was almost overwhelming.

"Daniel, you didn't have to—"

"I wanted to." He pulled a batch of golden cookies from the oven, the kitchen filling with the warm scents of molasses, ginger, and cinnamon. "Besides, it's Christmas Eve. Today should be special."

Grace stood on tiptoe to peek over his shoulder at the cookies, inhaling the beloved fragrance that brought back memories of her childhood home.

"They smell exactly right."

"Good." Daniel set the cookies on the counter to cool, then turned to face her. "Grace, there's something I want to ask you."

"Mrs. Clarkson mentioned that there's a special Christmas Eve service at the church tonight," Daniel continued, looking nervous. "I thought, well, I hoped you might like to go. Together, as a proper married couple."

Grace felt her heart swell. "I'd love that," she breathed.

Daniel's embrace was firm. "Grace, you're my wife, and I'm proud of that." The protectiveness in his voice made Grace's knees weak.

This was what it felt like to have someone willing to stand with her in marriage, and in life. Together they would stand against the world.

THAT AFTERNOON, Grace took special care with her appearance. She changed into her navy blue dress with the white collar and pearl buttons, and for the first time since arriving in Prescott, she felt beautiful rather than simply presentable.

Daniel appeared in the kitchen wearing his best suit, his hair neatly combed and his eyes bright with anticipation.

"You look lovely, Mrs. Carrington," he offered her his arm.

"So do you," Grace replied, meaning it. Her husband was a handsome man, and she was proud to walk beside him as his wife.

The ride to town was peaceful, the snow-covered countryside looking like something from a Christmas card.

Other families were heading to church as well, their wagons making tracks in the fresh snow.

Grace felt a sense of belonging. She was part of a community network, part of a family, and a part of something larger than herself now.

Families packed the little church, and the windows glowed against the winter darkness. Candles flickered on the altar, and pine boughs decorated the sanctuary, filling the air with the smell of Christmas.

Grace noticed several people look their way as they entered, smiling and nodding in welcome.

Mrs. Clarkson waved them over to sit with her family. "Grace, my dear! How lovely you look! That dress brings out your eyes."

Mrs. Foster nodded from across the aisle. "Mrs. Carrington, I do hope you'll consider joining our Christmas charity committee next year. We could use someone with your organizational skills."

Even Mrs. Whiteman, though she didn't speak to them, seemed to have found other targets for her attention.

Grace relaxed as she realized that time and her own behavior had won over many of the townspeople.

Reverend Shoemaker delivered a beautiful sermon about the gift of love and the importance of family, both born and chosen.

Grace thought about the journey that had brought her to this moment—from the devastating cruelty of her Uncle to the warmth of Daniel's love.

When the congregation rose to sing "Silent Night," Daniel's deep voice blended with Grace's soprano, and she felt tears of joy prick her eyes.

This was what she had always dreamed of finding. A true home, a loving partner, and a place where she belonged.

Back at the farmhouse, Daniel built up the fire in the parlor while Grace prepared hot chocolate and arranged the molasses cookies on their best plate.

The house felt cozy, decorated with the pine boughs and holly berries they had gathered in the nearby woods the week before.

"I have something for you," Daniel said, looking nervous again.

"I have something for you too," Grace replied, thinking of the warm scarf she had knitted in secret during the evenings when he thought she was mending.

"Ladies first," Daniel said, disappearing into their bedroom and returning with a small wrapped package.

Grace's hands trembled slightly as she unwrapped the gift. Inside was a small wooden jewelry box, beautifully crafted with intricate carved roses on the lid. She lifted the lid and gasped.

Nestled on a bed of blue velvet was a strand of perfect pearls, lustrous and warm in the firelight. They were like her mother's necklace but somehow more beautiful—rounder, more perfectly matched, with a clasp of delicate gold filigree.

"Daniel," she breathed, unable to find words.

"I know I can't replace your mother's necklace," Daniel said quietly, kneeling beside her chair. "Those pearls were irreplaceable because of what they meant and because of who gave them to you. But I wanted to give you pearls of your own. Pearls that represent our love and our future together."

Grace's eyes filled with tears as she touched the beautiful strand. "How did you? When did you?"

"I've been planning this since the day you told me about your mother's necklace," Daniel admitted. "I wrote to a jeweler in Kansas City for help. I wanted the pearls to be perfect for you."

With gentle hands, Daniel lifted the necklace from the box and moved behind Grace's chair.

"These pearls are a promise," he said as he fastened the clasp at the nape of her neck. "A promise that I love you, cherish you, and want you just as you are."

Grace touched the pearls at her throat, feeling their smooth warmth against her skin. But more than that, she felt the love behind the gift. Her husband's thoughtfulness, the care he took, and the understanding of what a pearl necklace meant to her.

"I love you," she whispered, turning to face him. "I love you so much, Daniel."

"I love you too," he replied, cupping her face in his hands. "My beautiful wife."

Later that evening, as they sat by the fire, with Grace wearing her new pearls and Daniel wrapped in the scarf she had knitted for him, Grace thought about the journey that had brought them to this moment.

"Do you know what I was thinking about during the service?" She asked, her head resting on Daniel's shoulder.

"What's that?"

"How different this Christmas is from what I expected when I left Boston. I thought I was being sent away because I was unwanted. I thought I would spend the rest of my life trying to earn my place in someone's home."

Daniel's arm tightened around her. "And now?"

"Now I know how it feels to be wanted. To be loved." Grace touched the pearls at her throat. "These aren't just a replacement for what I lost, Daniel. They're something entirely new. Something that belongs to our story."

“That’s what I hoped you’d understand,” Daniel said, pressing a kiss to the top of her head. “Grace, you’ve made me happier than I ever thought possible. You’ve turned this house into a home, and this life into an adventure.”

As the fire crackled and snow continued to fall outside their windows, Grace felt a deep sense of peace settle over her.

The scared, broken girl who had arrived in Kansas was gone, replaced by a woman who knew her own worth, who had found true love, and who looked forward to whatever tomorrow might bring.

“Merry Christmas, dear husband,” she whispered.

“Merry Christmas, Mrs. Grace Carrington,” Daniel’s voice was soft. “I love you.”

The firelight made the pearls gleam like stars against Grace’s throat, a symbol not of what was lost but of what was found.

Love given and received. A future bright with promise, and a marriage built on truth and trust.

Outside, the snow continued to fall, blanketing their little farm in pristine white. But inside, by the warmth of the fire, Grace and Daniel began the first of what would be many Christmas Eves together, celebrating in joy, as a family.

CHAPTER 21

MARCH 1886

The winter snow was finally melting, revealing the brown earth beneath and the first green shoots of spring pushing through the softened ground.

Grace stood at the kitchen window, watching Daniel repair the garden fence that had been damaged by the weight of ice during the February storms.

Her hand absently touched the pearl necklace at her throat—she had worn it every day since Christmas, finding comfort in its smooth warmth and the path forward it represented.

Three months had passed since that magical Christmas Eve, and their marriage had grown stronger with each passing day.

Daniel had been true to his word about supporting her dreams. Just last week, Miss Crawford had officially asked Grace to become her assistant at the school, starting after Easter.

Grace was looking forward to teaching the younger children, and finally putting her education to good use.

The sound of an approaching wagon drew her attention. A well-dressed young man was driving toward their farmhouse, and something about his careful posture and nervous energy seemed familiar.

As he drew closer, Grace gasped in recognition.

"James?" she muttered, her heart beginning to pound. "What in the world is Mr. Coleman's clerk doing here?"

Grace hurried outside, calling to Daniel. "Someone's coming! I think I know who it is. I think it's James, the clerk from the businessman's office back home."

Daniel dropped his hammer and strode quickly to her side, his expression alert.

The young man climbed down from the wagon, his city shoes sliding in the wet dirt. Clutching a leather satchel, he looked around the farm with apprehension.

"Grace Royce? Pardon me, Mrs. Grace Carrington?" James approached them with a respectful tip of his hat. "I'm James Fletcher, from Mr. Coleman's office in Boston. Grace, we met briefly before you left Massachusetts for Kansas."

"I remember," Grace said, her voice tight with alarm. "You delivered my train ticket to my home. What brings you all this way, Mr. Fletcher?"

"May we speak privately? I have some rather urgent business to discuss with you." James glanced at Daniel. "Though I believe your husband should hear this as well. It concerns your family's estate and certain criminal activities that have recently come to light."

Daniel stepped closer to Grace, his hand finding hers. "Let's go inside."

Seated around the kitchen table with coffee growing cold before them, James opened his satchel and withdrew a thick folder of documents. His young face was serious as he began his explanation.

"Mrs. Carrington, after you left Boston, Mr. Coleman became increasingly troubled by what he witnessed regarding your uncle's handling of your father's estate. He asked me to conduct a quiet investigation into the matter."

Grace felt Daniel's hand tighten around hers.

"What we discovered," James continued, "was far worse than Mr. Coleman suspected. Your uncle has been engaged in systematic fraud and embezzlement for the past year."

"What kind of fraud?" Daniel asked, his voice hard.

James pulled out a ledger and several official-looking documents.

"First, your father's debts were largely fabricated. Your uncle forged documentation to make it appear that your father owed substantial sums to various creditors. In reality, your father's investments were quite sound, and the estate should have been worth approximately thirty-five thousand dollars."

Grace felt the blood drain from her face. "Thirty-five thousand? Dollars?"

"Yes. Your uncle also sold your mother's jewelry collection for nearly two thousand dollars, claiming it was to pay debts that didn't exist. Furthermore, he pocketed the money from the sale of your family home and its contents, which was another nine thousand dollars."

Daniel was calculating quickly. "That's almost forty-five thousand dollars he stole from Grace."

"Precisely." James nodded grimly. "But there's more. We discovered that your uncle never paid any dowry to Mr. Carrington. The three hundred dollars he claimed to have sent was never transferred. It appears he simply kept that money as well, along with the money Mr. Carrington here sent for your train ticket. Mr. Coleman sent me to secure and deliver your train ticket once you left his office that day, as you remember. Mr. Coleman wanted you to travel in some semblance of comfort on your journey."

Grace stared at the documents spread before her, her mind

reeling. “My father was not deeply in debt from bad investments? My father did not die broke and on the verge of being destitute?”

James quickly pulled a piece of paper from his satchel and placed it in front of Grace. Drawing her attention to a series of column entries, he explained.

“Grace, your father was a very shrewd businessman. His investments were successful, and your father owned substantial assets. Upon his death, all of those assets transferred to you, his daughter and only child.”

“You’re telling my uncle stole it all?”

“Yes, he did,” James confirmed. "Mr. Coleman has been in correspondence with banks and law enforcement for months, gathering evidence. Last week, your uncle was arrested on charges of fraud, embezzlement, and theft. He's currently in jail awaiting trial."

Daniel's arm came around Grace's shoulders as she began to tremble. "He's been caught? He's actually facing charges?”

"Oh yes," James said with satisfaction. "The evidence is overwhelming. Mr. Coleman was very thorough. Your uncle will likely spend the next ten years in prison, if he's fortunate. Some of the charges carry even longer sentences."

Grace felt a mixture of relief and vindication wash over her. "I can't believe it. Uncle convinced me I was worthless, and only because that would allow him to steal everything...”

"Your uncle deliberately destroyed your self-worth to maintain control over you in order to seize your money,” James said gently. "It was a calculated cruelty designed to make you grateful for any scraps of kindness."

Daniel's jaw clenched with anger. "If I ever see that man..."

"You won't," James assured him. "He'll be locked away for a very long time."

James pulled out another set of documents, these bearing

official seals and ribbons. "This brings me to the second purpose of my visit. Mr. Coleman has been working with the courts to recover your stolen inheritance. We've managed to reclaim a goodly portion of it."

He handed Grace a bank draft, and her eyes widened at the amount written there.

"Twenty-six thousand, four hundred dollars," James announced. "That represents the partially recovered estate funds, some of the proceeds from the jewelry sale, the house sale, minus legal fees and Mr. Coleman's expenses for the investigation."

Grace stared at the bank draft, unable to process the number. "I don't understand. This much money?"

"There is approximately ten thousand dollars that will never be recovered, your uncle did abscond with that. Your father was a wealthy man, Mrs. Carrington. Your uncle's lies made you believe you were penniless, but you're actually quite well-off. This money, properly invested, could provide you with financial independence for the rest of your life."

The kitchen fell silent except for the ticking of the mantel clock. Grace looked from the bank draft to Daniel's face, seeing a complex mixture of emotions there—joy for her vindication, concern about what this meant for their marriage, and something that might have been fear.

"Daniel," she said softly, "what are you thinking?"

He was quiet for a moment, then said carefully, "I'm thinking that you now have choices you didn't have before. You could go anywhere, do anything. You don't need to stay here if you don't want to."

Grace felt tears prick her eyes at the vulnerability in his voice. Even now, after everything they'd been through, he was giving her an escape if she wanted it.

"James," she said, not taking her eyes off Daniel's face,

"would you excuse us for a moment? There's something I need to discuss with my husband."

James nodded and stepped outside on the porch, giving them privacy.

Grace rose from her chair and moved to stand before Daniel, taking his hands in hers. "Do you remember what you told me on Christmas Eve? About the pearls being a promise?"

Daniel nodded, his brown eyes serious.

"You said they were a promise that I was loved, cherished, and wanted exactly as I am." Grace touched the necklace at her throat. "Well, I have a promise for you too."

She picked up the bank draft and, without hesitation, tore it in half.

"Grace!" Daniel was horrified. "What are you doing?"

"Making a choice," she said firmly. "The same choice I made when I married you, when I learned to love you, when I decided this was my home. Money doesn't change that."

"But Grace, that's your inheritance, your security—"

"You are my security," Grace interrupted. "This farm is my home. Our life together is what I choose. I don't want to be anywhere else or with anyone else."

Daniel stared at her, his throat working with emotion. "Are you sure? You could have anything you wanted now."

Grace smiled, feeling lighter than she had in months. "I already have everything I want. But Daniel, I do have some ideas about how we could use this money to help the town. The school needs supplies, and there are families who struggle through the winters. Maybe we could even start a small lending library..."

Daniel's face broke into a wide grin, and he pulled her into his arms. "Have I told you lately that I love you, Grace Carrington?"

"Not in the last hour," she laughed, kissing him soundly.

When James returned, he found them seated close together at the table, the torn bank draft between them. His eyes widened in shock.

"Mrs. Carrington, what happened to the bank draft?"

"I tore it up," Grace said cheerfully. "But don't worry. I'd like you to help me arrange for the money to be transferred to the Prescott Bank. Daniel and I have plans for it."

"Plans?" James looked confused.

"Community improvements," Daniel explained, his arm around Grace's waist. "My wife has some excellent ideas about how to help our neighbors."

James slowly smiled. "Mr. Coleman said you were unique, Mrs. Carrington. I believe he understated the case."

As they worked out the details of transferring the funds and discussed Grace's ideas for community projects, Grace felt a deep sense of peace settle over her.

Uncle's lies had been exposed, justice had been served, and she had proven—to herself and to Daniel—that her love was genuine.

The scared girl who had knelt on Uncle's floor, gathering scattered pearls, was truly gone. In her place sat a woman who knew her worth, who had chosen love over money, and who was ready to use her blessings to bless others.

Later that evening, as James prepared to return to town to spend the night at the Cozart Hotel before beginning his journey back to Boston, Grace and Daniel stood on their porch watching the sunset.

The air was soft with the promise of spring, and Grace could hear the first tentative songs of returning birds.

"Do you have any regrets?" Daniel asked quietly.

Grace considered the question seriously. "About tearing up the bank draft? Not for a moment. About leaving Massachusetts? Not anymore. About marrying you?" She smiled up at him. "That was the best decision I ever made."

"Even though you didn't really make it? Your uncle forced you into it."

"Maybe Uncle arranged the circumstances," Grace said, "but I made the choice to love you. I made the choice to stay. I made the choice to build a life here. And today, I made the choice to put our marriage before money."

Daniel kissed the top of her head. "What did I do to deserve you?"

"You chose to love a difficult, defensive woman who came with more baggage than you bargained for," Grace replied. "You were patient when I was impossible, more than kind when I was hurtful, and faithful when I was faithless."

"And you," Daniel said, "transformed a lonely house into a home and a practical arrangement into the greatest love story I could have imagined."

As they stood together in the gathering dusk, Grace touched her pearl necklace one more time. Uncle had tried to break her spirit by scattering her mother's pearls across the floor, but Daniel had given her something even more precious—a love that was freely chosen, freely given, and strong enough to withstand any storm.

The pearls would always remind her not just of what she had lost, but of what she had found: a home, a partner, a purpose, and a future bright with promise.

Uncle's cruelty had been meant to destroy her, but instead, it had led her to the one place she truly belonged and a strength she didn't know she possessed.

Justice had been served, truth had prevailed, and love had conquered all. It was, Grace thought as Daniel took her hand and led her inside, the perfect ending to the story she had never expected to have—and the perfect beginning to the life she had always dreamed of living.

CHAPTER 22

CHRISTMAS EVE 1886

The fire crackled softly in the parlor hearth, casting dancing shadows across the walls of the farmhouse that had become Grace's true home.

Snow fell gently outside the frosted windows, just as it had exactly one year ago when Daniel had given her the pearl necklace that rested at her throat.

Grace rocked slowly in the wooden chair Daniel had crafted for her during the long autumn evenings, her heart full to overflowing as she gazed down at the sleeping infant in the cradle beside her.

Little Rose Carrington, named for the delicate embroidered roses Grace had stitched during their courtship, was two months old, with Daniel's dark hair and what Grace hoped would be her father's kind brown eyes. The baby's tiny fist was curled against her cheek, and Grace marveled again at the perfect miracle of her daughter.

"She's beautiful when she's sleeping," Daniel said softly, settling into his chair beside Grace with two cups of hot cider. "Almost makes you forget she kept us awake half the night."

Grace smiled, accepting the warm cup gratefully. "Mrs. Clarkson says all babies do that. She'll settle into a routine soon enough."

"Mrs. Clarkson also says Rose has your stubborn streak," Daniel teased, his eyes twinkling in the firelight.

"My stubborn streak?" Grace laughed quietly, mindful of the sleeping baby. "She gets that from both sides, I'm afraid. Have you forgotten who insisted on building a new school-house when the old one would have served perfectly well?"

Daniel grinned. The new Prescott schoolhouse, funded in part by Grace's inheritance and built by willing community hands, had been their first major project together.

Grace taught there three days a week, with Miss Crawford handling the older children while Grace worked with the youngest ones.

It was everything Grace had hoped for—a way to use her education to benefit their town of Prescott while still being home for Rose.

"Do you remember last Christmas Eve?" Grace asked, settling back in her chair as Rose stirred slightly but remained asleep.

"Every moment of it," Daniel replied, reaching over to touch the pearl necklace at Grace's throat. "The night you finally believed that you were wanted, and knew you were loved. The night we stopped being strangers and became husband and wife."

Grace's hand covered his. "I was thinking about everything that's happened since then. James's visit, Uncle's arrest, the money..."

She paused, looking around their comfortable home. "But most of all, I was thinking about how grateful I am that we found each other."

The past year had indeed been full of changes. Grace's inheritance had allowed them to expand the farm, add a proper dairy operation, and hire two steady workers who lived in the new bunkhouse Daniel had built.

But more importantly, it had given them the resources to help their neighbors. Together they had partially funded the new school and established a small lending library.

“The town council wants to name the library after you," Daniel said with pride. "The Grace Carrington Memorial Library."

"It's not a memorial if I'm still alive to use it," Grace protested, though she was touched by the gesture. "Besides, it should be named after Father. He's the one who taught me that education was the most valuable gift you could give someone."

Daniel's expression grew tender. "He would be proud of you, Grace. Of the woman you've become and of the difference you're making in Prescott.”

"Speaking of gifts," Daniel said, his voice taking on a familiar note of nervous excitement that Grace had learned to recognize. "I have something for you."

Grace's eyebrows rose. "Daniel Carrington, we agreed no gifts this year except for Rose's first Christmas dress."

"This isn't exactly a new gift," Daniel said mysteriously, reaching into his pocket. "It's more like... finishing an old one."

He pulled out a small velvet box, but this one was different from the jewelry box he had given her the year before. This was smaller, older-looking, and Grace's breath caught as she recognized the faded blue velvet.

"Is that...?"

"The box your mother's jewelry came in," Daniel confirmed. “Mr. Coleman found it among some things your uncle left behind when he fled town. He thought you might want it back."

Grace reached out with trembling fingers to touch the familiar carved rosewood. It was the box Uncle had forced open and ransacked, the one that had been knocked to the floor during their terrible confrontation. Seeing it again brought back a flood of memories—both painful and dear.

"Open it," Daniel said gently.

With careful hands, Grace lifted the lid. Inside, nestled on a bed of new blue velvet, was the most beautiful hair comb she had ever seen. It was crafted of silver filigree, delicate as lace, and set into its elegant curves were five perfect pearls—pearls she recognized immediately.

"Daniel," she whispered, her eyes filling with tears. "How did you...?"

"The five pearls you saved," Daniel explained softly. "The ones you sewed into your dress lining. Please, look at the clasp."

Grace lifted the comb from the box with shaking hands. The silver clasp that held the comb's teeth together was fashioned from a piece of ornate metalwork that made her heart skip.

"The clasp from Mother's necklace," she breathed. "You had it made from the original clasp."

"The jeweler in Kansas City is very skilled," Daniel said, watching her face carefully. "He was able to incorporate both the pearls and the original clasp into something new. Something that honors your mother's memory while being uniquely yours."

Grace turned the comb over in her hands, marveling at the craftsmanship. The five pearls were arranged like tiny stars against the silver, and the original clasp had been transformed into an elegant centerpiece. It was as if her mother's scattered treasures had been reborn into something even more beautiful.

"I don't understand," Grace said, though her heart was already beginning to comprehend the depth of Daniel's thoughtfulness. "When did you...? How did you go about doing this?”

Daniel's cheeks reddened slightly. "The night you told me about trying to find your mother’s pearls on the floor, you were so upset you didn't notice when I told you that someday we would find a way to honor them properly."

Grace was crying now, but they were tears of joy and over-whelming love. "Daniel, this is... I have no words. It's perfect."

"Your mother's pearls," Daniel said softly, “and a new life in our home, in our family. The past and the present joined together, just like us."

Grace carefully pinned the comb into her hair, where it caught the firelight and seemed to glow with an inner warmth.

Rose stirred in her cradle, opening her dark eyes as if she sensed the importance of the moment.

"Now she's awake," Grace laughed through her tears, lifting their daughter into her arms. "As if she knew it was time to see Mama's Christmas gift."

Daniel moved his chair closer, wrapping his arms around both his wife and daughter. "Do you know what I see when I look at that comb?"

"What do you see?"

"I see the strength you inherited from your mother. I see the love that survived even when pearls were scattered and dreams were broken. I see a woman who took the fragments of her past and built something beautiful for her future."

Daniel kissed the top of Grace's head, just above where the comb nestled in her hair. "And I see our daughter's inheritance—not just pearls and silver, but the story of a mother who chose love over fear, who chose family over money, who chose to believe in the love of her husband.”

As Grace sat surrounded by her family, the pearl comb in

her hair and her baby daughter in her arms, she thought about the journey that had brought her to this moment.

From the terrified girl gathering scattered pearls on Uncle's floor to the confident woman building a new life with her chosen family—it seemed like a lifetime of change compressed into a little over a year.

"What are you thinking about?" Daniel asked, noting her thoughtful expression.

"I'm thinking about stories," Grace said softly, adjusting Rose's tiny blanket. "About how every broken thing can be made beautiful again if you find the right person to help you put the pieces back together."

"And what story will you tell Rose about her hair comb?" Daniel asked.

Grace looked down at her sleeping daughter, then up at her husband's loving face. "I'll tell her it's made of dreams that survived heartbreak. I'll tell her it represents a love that was strong enough to gather scattered pieces and make them whole again. And I'll tell her that sometimes the most beautiful treasures come not from what we're given, but from what we choose to build with our own hands and hearts."

Outside, the snow continued to fall, blanketing their farm in pristine white. But inside, by the warmth of their fire and surrounded by their love, Grace Carrington held her daughter close and marveled at the perfect circle of her life.

The girl who had once believed she was worthless had become a woman who knew her infinite value. The scattered pearls had found their way home. And the broken dreams had been transformed into a reality more beautiful than anything she had ever dared to imagine.

As the clock struck midnight, marking the beginning of Christmas Day, Grace touched the pearl comb in her hair and smiled. This was her true inheritance—not the money Uncle had stolen or even the wealth that had been returned to her, but this moment, this family, this love that had grown from the smallest seeds of hope into something magnificent and enduring.

The circle was complete, and Grace Carrington had finally come home.

ABOUT THE AUTHOR

“Olivia Poe is an award-winning author with a knack for crafting clean and sweet historical and contemporary romances.

With a degree in History and a special emphasis on American history, she brings authentic detail to every story she tells.

Olivia is fascinated by the incredible women who traveled west to become mail-order brides. "It took an inner strength and belief in themselves that not many people possess,” she says. "I'm honored to be telling their stories."

When she's not writing about brave women finding love on the frontier, Olivia can be found researching forgotten corners of Americana, or planning her next escape to the coast or the mountains, and dreaming up new adventures for her characters.

She’s fond of saying she “... writes from the Midwest United States via side trips to Europe and the Seven Wonders of the World.”

~

Please sign up for Olivia’s newsletter!
Free books, swag boxes, first to know when a new book is published!
www.OliviaPoeFiction.com

~

Join us on Facebook and Instagram!

Check out more of my books on Amazon!

OliviaPoeBooks dot com

Welcome to the Olivia Poe Readers Group! We've created a fun place where readers can come together to share their love of reading and romance. Let's talk about good books, good food, this thing called life - and more!

https://www.facebook.com/groups/oliviapoereaders

instagram.com/oliviapoeromance#

facebook.com/oliviapoefiction

amazon.com/stores/Olivia-Poe/author/B011TN0W18?

SONG OF THE PRAIRIE HEART

When Boston schoolteacher Catherine Wells answers a widowed farmer's advertisement for a wife, she trades her comfortable life for the harsh Kansas prairie.

Conner McKenna needs help with his four grieving children, not love—but Catherine's gentle strength and the music she brings to their home begin to heal hearts he thought were beyond repair.

As Catherine struggles to win the children's trust and learn frontier life, she discovers that building a family requires courage, sacrifice, and faith.

When a devastating prairie fire threatens everything they've built, Conner must choose between practical survival and the one thing that has brought joy back to their lives.

A lovely historical romance about second chances, the power of music, and finding home where you least expect it.

~

CHAPTER ONE

Spring 1882, Kansas Frontier

The morning sun cast long shadows across the prairie as Conner McKenna stood in the doorway of his farmhouse, coffee cup in hand, surveying the chaos that had become his life.

In the distance, his wheat fields stretched toward the horizon in neat, promising rows—the one thing that still seemed to flourish under his care. Everything else was falling apart.

"Pa! Finn took my doll and threw it in the chicken coop!" Rebecca's shrill voice pierced the morning air, followed by the sound of her bare feet pounding across the wooden floor behind him.

Conner closed his eyes and took a long sip of the bitter coffee. Two years. It had been two years since Fern had died bringing their fifth child into the world—a son who had followed his mother into heaven before his first breath.

Two years of trying to be both father and mother to four grieving children while keeping the farm from ruin.

"Finn McKenna, you get yourself in here this instant!" Mary's voice carried the authority of someone far older than her fourteen years, but Conner could hear the exhaustion beneath it.

His eldest daughter had shouldered burdens no child should bear, and the weight was showing in the sharp lines around her eyes and the way her shoulders curved inward, as if protecting herself from the world.

The sound of eleven-year-old Finn's whooping laughter drifted in from the yard, followed by the irate squawking of disturbed chickens.

Conner knew he should intervene, should march out there and restore order with a firm hand the way Fern used to do with just a look. Instead, he found himself rooted to the spot, overwhelmed by the simple act of deciding which crisis to address first.

"Conner McKenna, you are a coward," he mumbled to himself, the words bitter as the coffee. Fern would have had all four children fed, dressed, and at their chores by now. She would have done it with a song on her lips and flour in her hair, making even the hardest days feel like blessings.

Five-year-old James appeared at his elbow, clutching his stuffed horse and looking up with eyes the same cornflower blue as his mother's. "Pa, I'm hungry."

The simple statement hit Conner like a physical blow. When was the last time he'd given proper thought to what the children needed for breakfast? Mary had been handling the cooking, but she was just a child herself, trying to manage tasks that challenged grown women.

"Of course you are, son." Conner set down his coffee and lifted James into his arms, feeling the solid weight of his youngest child against his chest. "Let's see what Mary's fixed for us this morning."

The kitchen told the story of their struggles in cracked dishes and surfaces that never quite seemed clean no matter how hard Mary scrubbed.

Standing by the wood stove, the girl stirred porridge, her blonde hair escaping her braid.

"The milk's gone sour again," she announced without turning around, her voice carrying a weariness that made Conner's chest tighten. "I tried to make the porridge with water, but it's not..." She trailed off with a helpless shrug.

Rebecca burst through the back door, her face streaked with dirt and tears. "He put my doll right in the nastiest part of the coop, Pa! Miss Lucy is all covered in chicken mess, and Finn said she belongs there 'cause dolls are stupid baby toys!"

Before Conner could respond, Finn appeared in the doorway, dirt under his fingernails and a defiant gleam in his eyes that reminded Conner of himself at that age. "She's too old for dolls. Ma would've said so."

The kitchen fell silent except for the bubble of Mary's porridge. The mention of their mother always did this—created a stillness that felt like holding one's breath, waiting for something everyone knew would never come.

Conner set James down and looked at each of his children. For the first time in a long time, he really looked at them.

Mary's dress was too short and bore stains that wouldn't come out. Finn's trousers had holes in both knees. Rebecca's hair hadn't seen a proper brushing in days, and little James clung to his stuffed horse like a lifeline because it was the only thing left that held memories of his mother.

"We can't go on like this," he cried, the admission scraping his throat raw.

Mary turned from the stove, her childish face creased with worry. "Pa? What do you mean?"

Conner met her eyes, seeing Fern's intellect and determination there, but also seeing something that should never exist in a fourteen-year-old's gaze—the weight of holding a family together and trying to be an adult.

"You children need so much more, you all deserve better than this. You need a proper home. Proper meals. Someone who knows how to..." He gestured helplessly at the surrounding chaos.

"We got you, Pa," Finn said, his earlier defiance melting into something smaller and more fragile. "We don't need nobody else."

But they did. Conner could see it in the way Rebecca's dress hung loose on her thin frame, in the exhaustion lining Mary's face, in the way James barely spoke anymore except to ask for things they couldn't provide.

They needed what he couldn't give them: a mother's touch, a woman's wisdom, and the kind of care that came instinctively to someone who understood the complex needs of children and a home.

That evening, after feeding the children more watery porridge and sending them to bed, Conner sat at the kitchen table with a piece of paper, a pencil, and the weight of a decision that felt both important and impossible. The words came slowly, each one carefully chosen:

> *Seeking a God-fearing woman of excellent character for companionship and household management. A widowed farmer with four children requires help to manage home and family. Must be of good moral standing and possess domestic skills. Matrimonial intentions honest and immediate. Correspondence welcomed.*

He stared at the words until they blurred, thinking of Fern and the way she'd light up when she laughed, how she'd hum while she worked, and the gentle patience she'd shown with each of their children.

No advertisement could capture what he'd lost, and no stranger could replace it. But perhaps someone could help him build something new from the ashes of what remained.

Read Song of the Prairie Heart

~

~

www.ingramcontent.com/pod-product-compliance
Lightning Source LLC
LaVergne TN
LVHW051003080826
845145LV00009B/2429

* 9 7 8 1 9 4 5 7 0 8 0 1 5 *